MOTHER INDIA

Praise for *Mother India*

'*Mother India* is literature written in the time of virality. Fiction against the fiction of fake news.'

— AMITAVA KUMAR, author of *My Beloved Life*

'Prayaag Akbar offers a chilling portrait of modern India, where viral images manipulate national politics. This is a landscape where objectification is mistaken for intimacy, where attention can often lead to violence. A brilliant and sharply drawn novel.'

— AVNI DOSHI, author of *Girl in White Cotton* (aka *Burnt Sugar*)

'An expansive, yet fine-grained, depiction of the ambitions, compromises and deceptions that make up life in India today, as well as a stirring reminder that our greatest technologies remain as yet in service to our most ancient instincts. Prayaag Akbar is a clear-eyed chronicler of India – both as it is and as it may one day be.'

— MADHURI VIJAY, author of *The Far Field*

'What happens inside the largest online hate factory network in the world is a question that has intrigued every one of us. *Mother India* offers us a gripping account of the alternate universe of post-truth trolls, and Prayaag

Akbar's empathy and precision provide the perfect counterfoil to the darkness that unfolds.'

— MEENA KANDASAMY, author of *Tomorrow Someone Will Arrest You*

'Tender and ferocious on the same page. This is a swift, thrilling journey into Modi's India's bowels.'

— MOHAMMED HANIF, author of *Red Birds*

'Set in the post-truth era, this powerful novel brilliantly captures how technology enables invisible connections without the explicit consent of the people involved, as violence and immorality are normalized by the poisoning of routine acts in everyday life. In its new-age tale we see that people crave a space for the human imagination to build sound relationships in a fast-paced world hungry for instant gratification. Prayaag Akbar depicts beautifully the nuances of the contemporary world, where success is characterized by speed, news by its viral quality, and love by demonstration.'

— VIVEK SHANBHAG, author of *Sakina's Kiss*

MOTHER INDIA

a novel

PRAYAAG AKBAR

FOURTH ESTATE · *New Delhi*

First published in India by Fourth Estate 2024
An imprint of HarperCollins Publishers
4th Floor, Tower A, Building No. 10, Phase II, DLF Cyber City,
Gurugram, Haryana – 122002
www.harpercollins.co.in

2 4 6 8 10 9 7 5 3 1

Copyright © Prayaag Akbar 2024

P-ISBN: 978-93-6213-332-8
E-ISBN: 978-93-6213-812-5

This is a work of fiction and all characters and incidents described in this book are the product of the author's imagination. Any resemblance to actual persons, living or dead, is entirely coincidental.

Prayaag Akbar asserts the moral right
to be identified as the author of this work.

For sale in the Indian subcontinent only

All rights reserved. No part of this publication may be reproduced, stored in a retrieval system, or transmitted, in any form or by any means, electronic, mechanical, photocopying, recording or otherwise, without the prior permission of the publishers.

Cover photographs: www.rawpixel.com, www.unsplash.com

Typeset in 12/17.2 Adobe Caslon Pro at
Manipal Technologies Limited, Manipal

Printed and bound at
Thomson Press (India) Ltd

For Shanta, my girl from the hills

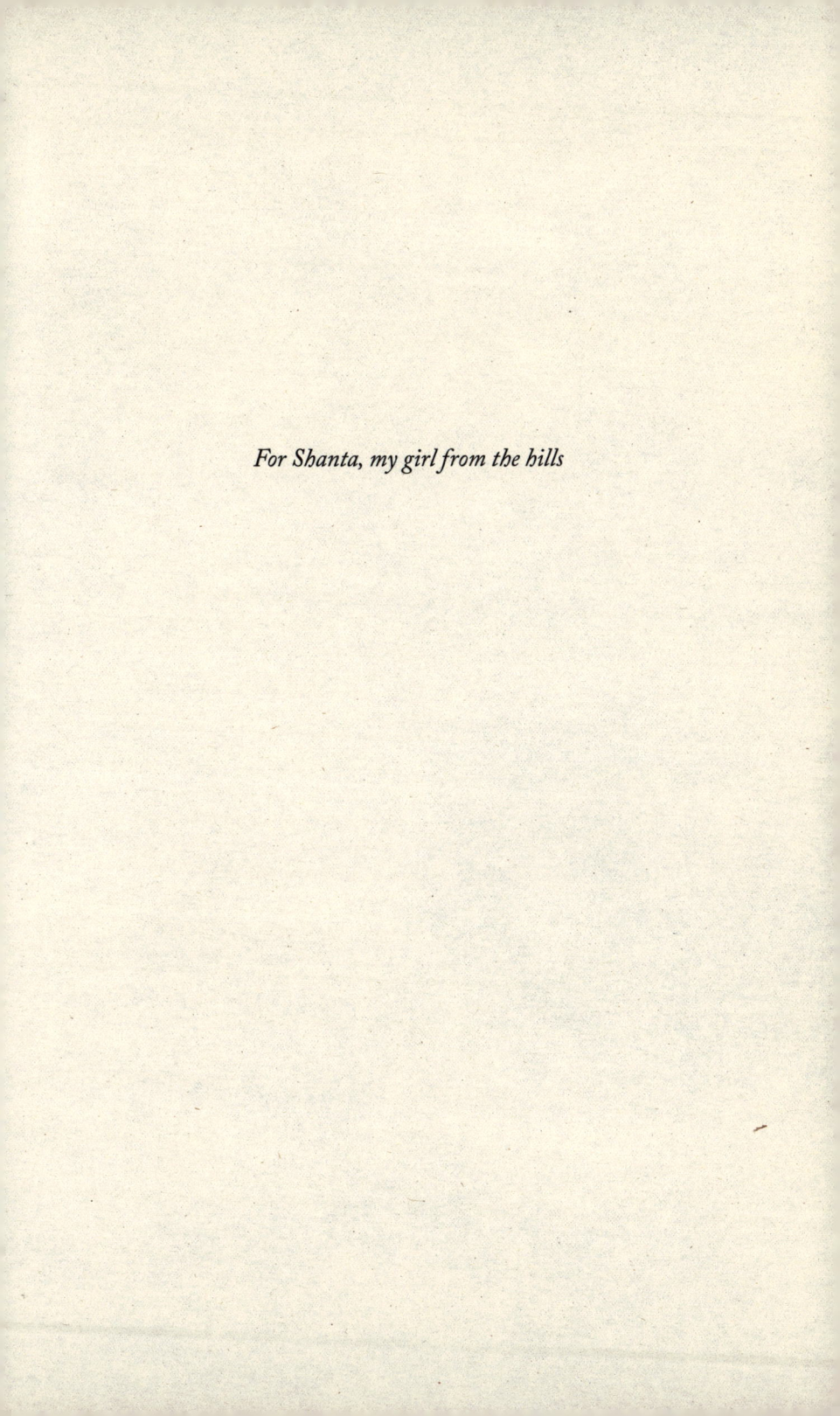

ONE

1

MAYANK WAS NOT PRONE TO falling in love. He liked to avoid such distractions. As he assured all who happened on his Twitter bio, appended, most recently, with three tricolour and one temple emoji, it was his nation he loved first. How he loved his country. When the anthem sounded before a World Cup game against the great enemy and the handsome old flag began to flutter and flick he'd feel a sure weight in his throat, as if pride had stopped his power to speak, and he'd have to fight back the ready drop that threatened to form at his eye. Yet here was today. This instant. A moment that seemed to pulse with the unmistakable message that he'd fallen feet first. The girl had a faraway look in her pale green eyes, dupatta demure around her head, an endearing mole, a light-brown diamond, on her left cheekbone. Strung around her as a canopy were hundreds of small and large metal bells darkened by age and swatches of thin red cloth with tasselled gold borders. The photograph had been taken at the Golu Devta temple. But where on earth was Ghorakhal?

Her bio gave little information save her age, twenty-three, and sign, Libra, the scales of justice rendered in a geometric symbol that Mayank remembered faintly from school and now looked up, falling briefly into a Wiki-hole explaining Euclidean equipollence. Once he emerged, confused and mildly regretful, he watched the first video Nisha had posted, set to a soft, rhythmic peal, a slow-motion clip shot from behind of her climbing the temple steps. He moved to the other video, self-recorded. In the thumbnail Nisha was standing in front of a small rough idol. The video began with a close-up, an awkward face, a fleeting moue that made his heart jump, and then she forgot the nervous start, speaking at a respectful whisper about the importance of this god. 'Jai Nyay Devta,' she intoned, four elegant fingertips placed delicately upon her sternum, and in her low throaty voice Mayank felt their connection burn afresh.

She hadn't posted for months. More than a year, actually. A couple of selfies, towards the bottom, one from a shining steel elevator, most likely at a mall, in which Nisha stuck the rosy tip of her tongue out awkwardly. He scrolled back to the series that had first corralled his attention, pausing at a close-up where she was leaning on a railing in front of a waterfall – geotag

Corbett Falls – just as a fine mist cascaded, producing a subtle consonance with her curls, free now of the dupatta's constraints. The picture had something of an other-worldly quality. Mayank noticed now that Nisha liked to look away from the camera as if something in the distance had drawn her interest – it was probably this that had reminded him of the source image. His boss had sent a link the night before. A painting by Tagore. But not, it turned out, the famous one. That guy's nephew, Abani-something.

'What do you think?' Mayank asked.

Sushil leaned over to consider the comparison. 'Isn't she a bit young?'

'In all the images I could find, she's young, Bharat Mata. Mother India is always painted young, never old.'

Sushil glanced at the plywood cabin that dominated the dark and dank basement in which they worked. 'Send the pics,' he shrugged. 'See what he says.'

In the cabin was their boss, Vikram Kashyap, a thirty-four-year-old who had acquired a measure of online celebrity, known for his waxy handlebar moustache and charmingly implosive turns of anger. Vikram was the procreator and host of *Kashyapji ka Right-Arm Fast*, a one-person discussion show on YouTube that had grown in six years to a substantial following. On air he spoke directly to the camera about any range of issues facing the country that day; coded in the camaraderie was the suggestion that he knew his audience shared his outlook, gender, rank, disposition. Kashyap favoured vexed, mocking expressions, drawing upon the internet's plenitude to scaffold his dark jokes, and it was towards this research that Mayank and before him Sushil had been recruited, foraging Reddit, 4chan and various other message boards for clips, memes, screenshots and other supporting material.

Sometimes Mayank's job demanded deep forays into Indian history. He found this amusing. After his tenths, when he was to choose his subjects for the last two school years, he'd asked for history, fine arts, psychology and economics. The principal summoned him to the office, informed him that he was wasting everyone's time, anyone with half a brain could see Mayank's only intention was to have his classes with the girls. Mayank took his place in the commerce stream, commencing a string of wretched struggles with calculus, and barely passed his school-leaving examinations.

His first job was at an event management company. Go in after parties at farmhouse weddings, collect the ashtrays and tiki torches, break down the tables, stack chairs, haul them to the trucks. He went by the title Service Event Assistant but the job felt a lot like manual labour. He worked for a while for a company called ScooterSerf, where he was a Delivery Executive. As he did not have a scooter he had to use his old bicycle, moving in long, sweeping circles around a little corner of the great city. He came to know the roads better. The muscles in his legs, shoulders and arms became incredibly hard, with little ridges and scarps in unusual places as if the muscles had muscles of their own, and the plates underneath his stomach tautened until they revealed themselves in the rough shape of a bar of chocolate. Sometimes he picked up lunch or dinner from a beautiful restaurant he could not before have imagined, a Chinese place with shimmering waterfall walls and enormous brass statues of the Buddha, an Italian cafe where you walked across a small footbridge inside the premises. In such places they didn't let him on to the restaurant floor. They kept him in the waiting area by the lectern at the front. As he exited, he would sneak a look at the bill of purchase, finding such figures that he even turned around once, convinced there was a mistake. But he came to admire the care such people took of their stomachs and their money. When he carried the bags of food to the magnificent homes to which they belonged, sprawling homes with sprawling gardens, the servant who came to the door never had a tip, and Mayank came to never expect any.

He kept his eyes open. Tried to understand without intimidation or envy these different places he was getting to see. Yet he would be overcome by a clammy mortification, sweat beading down his back, when he had to shoulder the insulated cube into his own neighbourhood. As his mother explained, in a somewhat strained tone, it is easy in this country to slip from the standing afforded by your community. Mayank could remember watching his father get dressed every morning in the bedroom mirror, his mother's red and black bindis reflecting on to themselves on one side of the mirror like soldiers facing off at a border. His father would comb his hair back and to the side with a pocket comb, tuck his shirt tight into the waistband of his trousers, adjust his belt, slowly scratch his trim stomach for reassurance. A government job, back when people could get such things. His father died on 12 July 2009. One among five in a chaos of imagined dust when a launching girder being used to build a bridge for the Delhi Metro collapsed. Mayank was nine. A couple of weeks after the funeral Mayank overheard his uncle tell his mother how lucky they were that it had happened while his father was on duty or the pension would've been half.

Mayank tried to experience his father's absence with a kind of dispassion, but it flared in his consciousness from time to time. How proud and strange and faintly green he'd felt with the winter cold tingling his upper lip and cheeks that first morning after shaving until a classmate had cackled during the morning assembly, pointing out in a whisper that Mayank had failed to negotiate the groove underneath his nose, that it looked like a dark, minute caterpillar was climbing out of one nostril and into the other. He worried that it made him selfish if he only felt his father's absence when he needed him. Now when people ask he speaks about his father's death and its impact in a forthcoming, unsentimental manner. Any sense of injustice he disguises. The memory is too big, perhaps, it does not need to be thought about very hard.

2

KASHYAP'S CABIN HAD A SET of black Indian clubs arrayed along one wall. He sometimes had the habit, while thinking through an idea, of pulling one down and striding around the office making helicopter twirls around his head, endangering the boys and various pieces of electronic equipment. Today the clubs were neatly in place, gleaming like granite.

On Kashyap's desk was the judge's gavel he'd been given by an admirer, engraved with his borrowed catchphrase, 'You can't handle the truth!'; also the silver plaque, awarded by YouTube, on reaching 100,000 subs. Now it was about the climb to a million, which sometimes did feel like a steep trek up to summit. You could see the peak, it wasn't far off, so you kept climbing, only to discover that the push you were hoping would take you all the way had only brought you to some kind of outcrop in the rock face.

'I've shared the images,' Mayank said. 'Please take a look.'

Kashyap picked up his tablet, scrolling slowly through the photographs Mayank had retrieved from the girl's feed. After some seconds, he said, 'Yes. Just what we need,' eyes intent upon the screen as if determined not to meet Mayank's gaze. Kashyap swallowed, a small stone emerging then retreating into his throat. 'Better make sure she's nobody.'

Mayank nodded his understanding. Yet he couldn't help but feel it was all a little strange. As ever, time was short. The AI kept mangling Mata's face. It had given her a weirdly planed nose, a fish mouth, one eye bigger than the other. If Mayank had to guess, he'd say it had something to do with the profusion of images out there. Bharat Mata, judging from the thousands of images buried in archival recesses of the internet, was the vision of pamphleteers, calendar makers, magazine and journal illustrators, people practising their skills at home, much of it way back in British time; not a profusion as much as a confusion of imagery, scarcely possible for this rudimentary AI to figure out.

He checked the portrait from 1905. Distant gaze, light-blue halo around her head, smear of bridal sindoor upon the apex of her forehead. Mother India. Her saffron sari was not tied in the fashion of a bride. She wore the outfit of a religious mendicant. Four arms, like a powerful goddess, each putting forth a gift to the nation: sheaves of paddy, a book, a rudraksha mala, a white duster. Mayank could not quite see how a new rendition of this tired old painting could inspire a fervour of patriotism amongst today's young people. Would they have to style her differently? It was easy enough to direct the program. He laughed, thinking of Blackpink hair, the powerful legs and upper body of a weightlifter, baggy distressed jeans, or a sari with a spangled blouse. He laughed once again. Kashyap would tear him a new one.

A bhajan floated up from a side table. It was followed quickly by another, as Kashyap's pair of impressive phones set up an insistent competition, like temples across a village pond. Mayank watched his boss evaluate each caller. Abruptly both noises were curtailed. Kashyap stepped out from behind his desk, large torso emphasizing the shortness of his legs, an effect that he counteracted with brightly coloured waistcoats buttoned tight around his waist.

'I didn't realize Bharat Mata is so young,' Mayank said. 'I thought she was an ancient symbol. But on Wiki they're saying barely one hundred years.'

'Not many people know,' Kashyap said. 'It started in Europe. When their countries were forming. Britannia. Germania. Always a woman.'

Mayank thought about this for a second. 'But we've all seen Bharat Mata so many times. On TV. Textbooks. How can she go viral today?'

Kashyap took a deep breath, and when he spoke his voice had shifted to a fluent resonance that was familiar from the show. 'She's sleeping. She first woke up a hundred years ago, when the British were stopping her from becoming who she is. Now she's under attack from inside. From PhD-waale. Jihadis. Khalistanis. Maoists and missionaries. They don't know her power comes from those who doubt. That she's strongest when she's attacked. We have to remind our countrymen she's under attack. Our mother! When she wakes, she'll show her full fury.'

A shadow fell into the room. Mayank's eye moved to the clerestory window, small and smudged and spotted, the basement's solitary source of natural light. A vendor's cart had settled in front of it but he could hear the creaks and cries of the market.

All morning a tension had revolved under the low ceiling. Kashyap would walk out of his cabin, silver Sennheisers slung on his neck, pacing the length of the floor in the dramatic way he favoured when he was about to launch into one of his speeches. Then he would swivel, slamming the door on his way back inside. They heard him promise very loudly that he would turn an unknown party's mother and sister into one entity. When he appeared at his doorway he was grinning dangerously.

'How fucking dare he?' Kashyap said. 'I'm going to roast that bearded bastard. Him and all his Commie buddies.'

Immediately Mayank understood what was tormenting his boss. Late last night the head of the student union at Jawaharlal Nehru University had given a fiery speech. A video of the event made it to Twitter and from there exploded on to all the platforms, sometimes only as snippets. Mayank watched the whole thing. The speech began as a routine update on some matters related to admissions, final submissions, the canteen. Then a faction of flag-bearing students suddenly appeared. 'Bharat Mata Ki Jai,' they chanted. 'Bharat Mata Ki Jai.'

Mayank could not understand why this simple chant seemed to rile up so many lefties. Why exactly did some people have a problem with hailing the motherland? It made him angry. Muslims, he knew, did not like to say it. They thought it would prevent entry into their heaven of waiting virgins. But it wasn't as if they were being forced to say 'Jai Shri Ram', as in other videos that had gone viral recently. A street-cart vendor, a homeless person, some waif of a man caught in a barrage of shoving and swearing. 'Jai Shri Ram,' a half-dozen toughs would force the Muslim to say. When they watched such videos, Kashyap and Sushil would quietly exult, but Mayank always felt thrown a little out of balance: the white light bright upon the man's face, his Adam's apple ducking in and out of sight in fear, trembling cheeks, pleading implanted in the eyes. Mayank wanted justice for his people. For his country. This felt a bit like bullying.

The video featuring the student union leader ended in something approaching a brawl as two groups of perhaps twenty pushed against one another like clashing currents. Plastic chairs brandished overhead. The new arrivals had become incensed when the student union leader, who came from an embattled region of Jharkhand, refused to take up their chant. 'I won't say it,' he said clearly into the microphone, his dark face hardly visible behind his beard. 'Your Bharat Mata doesn't look like my mother. I won't say Bharat Mata ki jai.'

Pandemonium. Camera suddenly unstable like an earthquake has hit. Dust, shouting, fists. The factions had threatened each other, then presumably sauntered off to their own holes on campus. Mayank did not properly understand what happened on campuses. He could only summon impressions from movies, which were of no practical use. How did colleges actually work? You could ruck like this and then next morning meet peacefully at the dining hall? Go to class together?

Kashyap cleared his throat. 'Back in British times, patriots used to spread her image on calendars. Now we have social media. Just look at the data. The crucial thing, the most crucial thing, is how to frame the question. *Do you respect my mother?* If he disrespected our mother, if they dared to disrespect our mother, they're going to have to pay.'

3

THE LIVING ROOM LIGHT WAS on. Mayank unlocked the door to his flat, the muscles along his right shoulder twitching, to see set out on the dining table three bowls of food lidded by plastic plates which when raised released a rain of vapour. Saag-chicken, paneer, pulao. Friday feast. He glanced gratefully at the closed door. His mother must've tried to wait up, he realized, because everything was still hot.

Propping his phone against a water bottle after he'd wiped it down, he opened Captain Flight's new post and ate until he could not, going back for more pulao, stripping the bones with his incisors, his right knee jogging in contentment. A glass of cold water, then another. Now he leaned back in his chair and for an instant Mayank allowed a clarified form of weariness to swim over him. He could always wake early tomorrow to finish up. Yet almost immediately he saw the futility.

Kashyap's deadline would anyhow keep him awake. Slowly he rose. Took the bowls into the overfull fridge, scooping the green-tinged bones and cartilage into a plastic container. Then he washed his plate in the kitchen sink along with his hands and mouth.

At the foot of the sofa he found the neatly folded bedsheets his mother had left. For most of his life Mayank had slept on a single-bed mattress on the floor here in the living room, but last year his mother and he had split the seventy-three hundred rupees required to purchase a Solis Primus sofa-bed, heavily discounted on Flipkart. Now he could stretch as he slept. This felt something like an indulgence; every morning he woke up hunched to the wall, whether out of habit or guilt. He opened out the sofa, stacking the day-cushions into a makeshift table upon which he placed the office laptop.

Most representations Mayank found had Bharat Mata imposed on the map of the country. She stood with her feet together at the bottom of the peninsula, arms reaching out so that her body became the body of the nation. Her torso appeared over the Gangetic plain, the sari or sometimes her tresses flowing as the great river would. The haloed head and mysterious placid face were invariably positioned over the northern reaches: Kashmir.

Mayank had now thought about this portrayal all day, and he was quite in awe of the first unknown artist who had painted her in this way all those years ago. She should be under attack, Vikram sir had specified. Mayank read the two-paragraph brief once again. He had already inserted the drawings of two young boys in ratty kurta pajamas on either side of the Mother's legs. The boys' right arms were bent at the elbow and raised over their heads. He placed white prayer caps on both their heads and rocks in their right hands. Now to animate them hurling these rocks at the body of the motherland. At first the rocks flew low, at the Mother's sari-clad knees, the Deccan plateau. More rocks towards the Gangetic plain torso and still more of these makeshift missiles landing on the gentle face over Kashmir. Mayank worked hard now, finessing the pleats of the sari, adding cartoonish flourishes to the blood that spurted each time a rock landed on the motherland's body. Once he was done he evaluated the four-second clip, and despite himself, as he watched, Mayank's chest began to tighten. His breath felt shorter. These two Muslim boys. Throwing rocks like they did at our soldiers in Kashmir. Against brave policemen when Babarpur and Gokulpuri went up in flames. Daring to raise their hand and voice against country. Against mother. Against all our mothers. The clip looped and the blood spurted and the rocks struck her legs and chest and arms just as they crashed upon the plateaus and mountains and rivers, the thighs and heart and angelic feet. He added an inspired flourish, a tiny flinch from Bharat Mata as a rock crashed into her cheek.

It was 1 a.m. Mayank stood and stretched. Some minutes ago, while he'd been finishing a delicate colour adjustment, there had been shouting out on the street. Mayank went to the window to investigate, looking down on to a tile shop that men sometimes gathered outside at night, once the shutters were down. Four or five scrawny men drinking. Bhojpuri film music. Construction labour. Migrants. He stared blankly out of the window, aware, dimly, of a small irritation to his calm that he could not place.

Two of the labourers commenced a kind of crouching dance, tumbling over and then springing back to their squat. Mayank picked up his phone and began to film them idly. You never know when you'll end up with viral gold. But the burst of alcoholic energy seemed to dissipate as soon as he started recording. There was a round of quiet laughter before the duo collapsed to the pavement. Mayank was still gawking absently at the street when he remembered the bones.

4

EITHER IT WAS THE METALLIC moan of the main door or they picked up his scent, charging up the steps yelping just as he stepped out into the chill night air. In the first lockdown Mayank had fed the mother, a mongrel with a collie's face and thick chestnut coat. When she got pregnant, he paid for a vet to take a look. She left him her litter at the foot of the staircase. When she occasionally reappeared now it caused the four pups great excitement. Mayank led them downstairs and squatted in the dust, letting the pups nip at his fingers. When he dumped the bones on the ground, a frenzy of growls and whimpers erupted as they nipped and climbed over each other.

He had tried social media. The post of the pup with the Hitler moustache went viral after a famous actress from South India retweeted it. He got lots of earnest comments, in the end nothing but a few more followers.

Instagram led to a visit from a family, a girl of seven or eight with her parents. They came in a Range Rover that could not fit in Mayank's lane, so he carried all four in a cardboard box to the main road. But the girl had a specific kind of dog in mind, something she'd seen on a TV show or in a film. They departed with guilty smiles. Mayank smiled to himself now, thinking back to Kashyap's flabbergasted expression when he'd asked if he could use the official account to post the puppy pictures.

A gleaming white sedan pulled up at the end of the lane. Mayank recognized the side panel of a soft-top C-class. His stomach plummeted. He considered dashing upstairs. But it would be more embarrassing if she saw him doing that. She stepped out of the car, adjusting her short silver skirt. Turned around and blew a kiss. The car sped off. Then she began to walk up the lane. Bhavna and Mayank had known each other since school. On a couple of occasions they'd taken things further. He thought they'd ended on good terms, but she hardly spoke to him now. Whatever. Captain Flight said it was better for a woman to hate you than to have no opinion at all.

This wasn't the first time he'd seen Bhavna dropped off late at night in a fancy car. His mother and the aunties on their road had also noticed. An ugly, vintage word came to mind. Yet Mayank paid close attention as she walked by the migrant labourers, in case one of them uttered something. This was still his neighbourhood. Anyway, Bhavna would scream right back at them, he was sure. No way she was going to accept nonsense.

She hadn't seen him so he could look openly. The hair was shorter. What exactly had happened between Bhavna and him? He only remembered how dissatisfied he felt towards the end. There were so many amazing girls out there. On Captain Flight's channel, in the videos and the comments below, they called boys like him a simp. Submissive. Women hated that. They certainly didn't respect it, no matter what they said. They respected men in C-class Mercs who dropped them at the end of the road and zoomed away, not some little boy who squatted in the dust with puppies. As soon as Mayank thought this he stood up manfully. He tried to scatter the pups with his boot, but they thought he was playing a game and began to nip at his ankles. This was how Bhavna came upon him, hopping on one leg as a three-month-old clung with all her jaw strength to the denim hem of his fraying pants.

'Need some help?' she asked. Was there something condescending in her smile? Like she was comparing this moment, comparing him, in fact, to the nightclub, the car ride, the exciting places she'd just come from. But as she stepped towards him her expression shifted, or perhaps it was a deceit of the light, and she looked suddenly warm, welcoming.

'Fun night?' Mayank asked in response. He could hear the slash of bitterness in his own voice.

'Not bad,' she said as she walked by. Mayank watched her cheeks shift underneath her shimmering skirt. She had strong shoulders and an upright gait, her head high. Suddenly an afternoon came back, the back row of a movie theatre, the crevices on that lovely, proud neck smelling of watermelon. 'Remember Rohit, from our class?' she called out over her shoulder.

The Gaur kid. Dull type. A boy of no consequence until his father converted the family land into a string of commercial properties along the national highway that became factory outlets for brands like Skechers and Hidesign. Now Rohit worked out at the Radisson. Changed cars every few months. They'd heard his father was opening a nightclub in AeroCity.

It didn't matter, not really, Mayank thought. It wasn't like the old times, like how his parents knew it. Nowadays a girl like Bhavna could do what she wanted. That ugly word popped into his head once more. But he knew not to make the mistake. In class 11 one boy had sent a video to his ex-girlfriend, a quick rap that compared her to a prostitute. He later claimed he was trying to make her laugh. Why else would he say she was frigid, that clever little rhyme with 'thandi'? But the girls in school were having none of it. They'd formed a WhatsApp group of their own. Soon the boy was completely ostracized.

Bhavna had almost reached her building, a four-floor structure with a collapsed boundary wall a little way down the lane.

Mayank cleared his throat. 'Real men don't need a car to get a girl,' he called out.

Bhavna laughed, turning. 'You going to give me a ride on your cycle? Where's your uniform? That colour suited you.' She had stopped now, her eyes shining, a wide smile that she tried to contain by biting down on her lower lip. Mayank felt an incipient thickening, an uncoiling.

He smiled back cheerily. 'If you want a ride, I can always find the right gear. There's all kinds of rides we can go on.'

She laughed again, a laugh that sounded like an invitation, a promise. 'You stay at Fun 'n' Food Village,' she said as she stepped over the threshold, 'I'm heading to Disney World.' She gave him a wink. Then she was gone.

Mayank said goodbye to the pups and walked whistling up the stairs, suddenly not tired. One more animation for the video tomorrow. He'd completed the first half of the clip. For the second half, the plan was to introduce the student union leader. He would acquire a scared face and suddenly rocket off-screen. He would be replaced, in a slow fade-in, by a benign, placid Prime Minister of India. The Prime Minister would bow his head and fold his hands before Nation and Mother. One last nuance from Kashyap: 'The boys throwing rocks,' he'd said, 'the student union leader, make sure they're quite small compared to the country. They have to be dwarfed. Tiny. But the Prime Minister has to be much bigger. Not the same size as Bharat Mata, but close, okay? Almost equal.'

5

HIS WAKING THOUGHT WAS NISHA. He was worried for her safety. Slowly the dream came back. A group of men were following her and as she moved she suddenly shifted into a sari. That was all he got. He pushed the back of his neck into his pillow in frustration, hearing, now, his mother in the kitchen clicking the gas lighter repeatedly. The blue flame whooshed up. A sharp inevitable aroma of roasting mustard filled his nostrils and soon enough the living room.

A memory surfaced. His mother's fingers upon a shirted shoulder. Without intending it the memory grew, almost as a dream, and just as a dreamer can pass like a spirit through the barriers before them Mayank could feel himself suddenly in that close room that smelled of wool, static and body odour. The wooden wall clock shaped like a map of India. The warmth of the glowing phone screen as it protected the little boy from the wolves and the world. The look of shock on his mother's face as she hauled him to his feet, tight, pinched, hurt visible through the dupatta she had used as a veil, though the face turned into another almost immediately, Chikoo, who lived in the next building, three years older, sharp mouth and nose crunched up in lascivious righteousness, almost like a beak, it seemed now, a beak that had squawked to everyone in school and would warble comments as he walked down the road, Chikoo who'd made a hell of the years that followed. Mayank squirmed under the sheets. Then he jumped out of bed, hoping to chase the thought away. But some trace of grievance must have lingered. For once he did not put away his bedsheets or fold his bed back into the sofa. He left them lying there and went into the bathroom.

After he had bathed he felt calm. The bedclothes had been put away. His mother was still in the kitchen. She gave him a wet-eyed smile, the shisham spindle of the madhani rolling smoothly from between her palms to the tips of her fingers, turning the bowl of curd on the counter to a churn of froth and foam. Mumma refused to use the mixie for his morning lassi. She claimed it affected the taste.

'So late you were yesterday,' she said.

'We're posting a new video tonight,' Mayank said. 'Lot of last-minute stuff.'

'Pass me a glass,' she said, pointing with her chin to the cupboard above the sink. 'I heard you go out again later.'

'With the bones,' Mayank said. He kept his face in the cupboard out of embarrassment and said hesitantly, 'Saw that Bhavna coming back, while I was outside. Some boy dropped her off.'

For seconds his mother did not say anything, he could only hear her working. When he turned, she said, 'Is that any time to come home?'

Even the aunties from the neighbourhood who gossiped about Bhavna with his mother would land, in a roundabout way, on her behaviour. What they imagined of it, Mayank thought with a smile. The solidarity of women, in this regard, was contingent upon the conventions they had absorbed in their own youth, certainly in terms of what they found permissible. He suddenly remembered Nisha again, and then the video.

'Our video this time is on Bharat Mata,' Mayank said. 'About mother and country. I think you'll like it.'

She took the proffered glass in hand and poured the lassi straight into it from the pouting scuffed-silver lip of the bowl, creating a creamy waterfall that grew and shrank in length. As Mayank drank, she said, 'Don't send it to me if that man is only shouting. I can't understand why he needs to be so angry.'

6

VIKRAM SIR HAD A BIT of the hobbyist about him. This fact had dawned on Mayank over the course of some months, as he noted a stream of arrivals from Amazon, each promising great things: a U-shaped aluminium device that enlarged and strengthened the wrist, a grainy supplement powder that replaced all your needed vegetables, a Made-in-India drone with a tricolour remote, swatches of electrostatic microfibre that were for a while the only things Sushil and he were allowed to use when wiping the screens in the office. After a lively video they'd made about bulldozer justice went super-viral Kashyap bought a conference table with a whiteboard surface that could double as an oversize standing desk, descending to crouching height at the touch of a button. Mayank smiled to himself, thinking back. The table had been imported after a fulsome recommendation from an American tech influencer. Unlike his own generation, who instinctively knew, Kashyap belonged to an age that could not always discern sponsored posts from uncorrupt recommendations. At any rate, their boss insisted they use the table at every opportunity, and it was around this that they sat now to hammer out the script that would accompany the Bharat Mata video.

Kashyap picked up the printout, cleared his throat, and began to read. 'And what next, now, for the Student of the Year? The Vriddha Vidhyarthi?' He looked around the table. 'That's good, isn't it? Funny?'

'Do people know what vriddha means?' Mayank asked. 'We don't want the joke to get lost.'

'Maybe it would be funnier in English,' Sushil said. 'Our Ageing Academic?'

'Nothing wrong with a little Sanskrit,' Kashyap said. 'And when I say Student of the Year, I want a flash of the movie poster, Alia's body with this fucker's face photoshopped. Okay? Get a good one. Bikini, miniskirt, something like that.' He stubbed a finger at the printouts in front of him, indicating the student union leader's swarthy, bearded face. 'Fair and lovely we'll make him.'

Mayank nodded, scribbling a note in the margins of his own printout of the script. Assuming his YouTube voice once again, Kashyap read, 'Student of the Year says he does not love Bharat Mata. Of course, this makes sense. Why should he love Bharat Mata? What has

Bharat Mata ever given him? Now, my dear viewers, I have been doing a little research of my own, and I can say without doubt that Bharat Mata has done nothing for our student leader. His father was uneducated, a child of landless farmers. But through the caste quota that we have in this country, he got a job at a government office. That may be so, but you must remember, Bharat Mata has done nothing for our Student of the Year. What, what, what is it?' he broke off, irritated, giving Sushil a fierce look.

'I was just thinking about that video we did last year,' Sushil said. 'About caste quotas. Aren't we against reservations? You said it doesn't help anyone. Now you're saying it helped his family?'

'On the whole it doesn't help anyone,' Kashyap said smoothly. 'For society it does not help. But this is something else. Let's not worry too much ... *When our Student of the Year was just a little boy, only five years old, he was enrolled in the village school. Soon he was selected to go to a special school in the district. A government school built for people like him. After graduation, he went to the state university. Here he studied Indian history, achieving high marks. He got admission, for his PhD, to the most prestigious, most leftist university in all of India. And now – at just twenty-nine years of age, at the young age of only twenty-nine –*

he is about to complete his studies. Why should someone like this care for Bharat Mata? What has our mother given him, after all? Twenty-nine years old and never had a job but what has this country given him? Nothing at all. Who are we to force him to say such a thing? He has never taken anything from Bharat Mata, has he? Why should he do pranam to her?'

Over the past year Mayank had spent a fair bit of time coursing about the internet for ways to improve his finances. In the main he browsed websites targeted at college-leaving students: sites that allowed you to upload your résumé for free, throwing up remote jobs based in America, that offered useful tips for job interviews, helped compare pay grades and work options across industries. To keep you coming back these websites also carried blog posts with query–retort titles like 'What Are the 16 Career Clusters? Definition and Guide' or 'What Are T-Shaped Skills? (And Why They Are Important)'. On one such site he came across an article headlined '26 Common Logical Fallacies to Avoid When Making an Argument'. This article fascinated Mayank, perhaps because of the nature of his workday. He made careful notes that he then transferred to Google Slides. On previous occasions he had identified when Kashyap was launching an ad hominem attack, a technique his boss seemed to favour, when he was resorting to an appeal to popularity or an appeal to emotion, when he had deployed circular reasoning or hasty generalizations. Mayank always kept these observations to himself. This time, he suddenly realized, Kashyap had used the straw man. There was more than exaggeration here. There was alteration.

Perhaps Mayank was riding high on the praise he'd received that morning for his work on the animation, because he decided to venture his opinion. 'Vikramji,' he said softly, 'I had just one question.'

'Say,' Kashyap ordered.

'Isn't it that this guy, in his speech, he said he loved the country? It was only this one symbol that he felt was not appropriate. So the education, reservation, all that … he isn't talking about that. Why don't we just stick with Bharat Mata? We can challenge him by explaining to our audience how important she is to us. Why we feel so much for her. Why we sing Bharat Mata Ki Jai.'

Kashyap leaned back in his chair as he considered this proposition. He looked briefly at Sushil and then settled his gaze upon Mayank, whose neck felt hot and began to itch. Then Kashyap threw himself forward, plonking his elbows on the conference table. 'You know, sometimes I really don't understand you two,' he said. Sushil glared at Mayank. 'So long you've been working for me now. But you haven't picked up the basics. It doesn't matter what he is saying. What he's actually saying or trying to say. It matters how *we* interpret it. We are the ones with the audience. What matters is how we relay it to our followers. What we make of his words so our followers click on the video. It's a jungle out there, men. Everyone eats. To make an impact on the internet you don't need ideas, you need enemies.'

TWO

1

NISHA BISHT SPOTTED THE STAIN in the bathroom mirror of the second floor of Empirium Mall, two tremulous streaks of lime green and a parallel dusting of brown on a shoulder sticky and fibrous with chlorophyll and mud. For a few seconds she stared in horror. Only twenty minutes until they opened. She messaged her manager, Siddharth, then turned to Google. A WikiHow suggested isopropyl alcohol. Nisha folded the jacket, stuffed it in her backpack, ran in shirtsleeves and heels along the enormous oval corridor that looked down upon the central lobby of the mall until she came to a small grey door adjunct to an elevator bank. Inside the room it was dark. Suddenly silent. A moistness in the air like clothes had been dried there. Now she breathed easier, although she still cursed herself for the decision taken yesterday after work, lured by a dramatic saffron sky to halt for a few selfies at the hillocky lawn outside the mall. She scooped up the big white plastic bottle that was on the shelf behind the janitor's blue bucket. To get the liquid into the fabric Nisha would have to sacrifice the toothbrush she always carried, in a small pouch in her backpack, along with a can of deodorant, make-up, hair clips.

The alcohol evaporated fast but it made Nisha's jacket smell of nail polish remover. She walked back along the corridor, patting the jacket without much hope to dry the water, on through the doors of the store, taking a second now to look about, find her feet, tug the wrinkles from her dress, fiddle with a strand of hair. It was only when she felt neat and complete, if still breathing slightly heavily, that Nisha nodded at the two young men who stood there in similar outfits of eggshell khaki. Siddharth smiled back and walked to the front to fling the double doors open.

The first arrivals to the building were usually college students, bunking class and there for the air conditioning, a population the mall's management was loath to keep out though they did not spend, and despite the fact that Nisha was not much older she'd already begun to see them through a faint tint, adopting the term her colleagues used, lobbywaale, because they almost never travelled to the higher floors. During lobbywaale hour the employees of Dojuri were rarely disturbed, a narrow band of fallow time when aromatic traces of roasted cocoa melded with lo-fi electronica and Nisha imagined herself as a marble statue sinking slowly into the plush carpet. When they weren't looking, Nisha studied the faces either side of her. The new guy seemed to be itching for his phone. The glass wall to the store created a goldfish bowl effect, which meant that mobile devices were strictly prohibited. Siddharth, as usual, looked impeccable, hair climbing one side like a wave, chest strong under his suit jacket. But it was Nisha who had a way of attracting the customer's eye. A few weeks after she joined, Siddharth conceived of a new rotational system they would have to follow on the shop floor. They all worked on commission, he said, so everything had to be totally fair.

Not that the first weeks had been easy. Almost every day she remembered a moment of mortification: The owner's college-going niece, just flown in from Mumbai, hook nose, warm smile, careless tattoos, dead phone that needed a charge. Nisha had produced an aberrant *bettery*, not just the once, and the girl had giggled, then covered her mouth, apologizing. A few seconds later, she'd whispered, 'Just so you know, it's pronounced *bat*-tery.' Nisha had nodded mutely, smiling though it burned behind her eyes. But she'd made it past that period, she thought grimly. Worked on herself.

Today her feet were encased in low-heel mules she'd bought online. How young and foolish she'd been when she first got here. Every day wearing a pair of high peep-toes that gave shape to her calves, revealing dainty tips she'd painted in a dark polish to match her uniform. By evening her heels and the arch of the right side hurt so much that she began to carry a tennis ball to work in her bag, using the back room and her break to roll out her feet, placing the sphere under her heel and then sinking her body weight upon it, rolling it inch by inch towards the base of her toes, making the muscle softly crackle, at least that's how it seemed in her head, each pop delivering its own blessed measure of release. Now she alternated between these mules and a strappy pair of platforms and every evening once home performed a twenty-minute YouTube yoga routine: an American woman on a balcony overlooking a wintry lake, a sequence, the caption claimed, designed especially for retail workers.

A tall man wearing a baseball cap, shorts and plain white T-shirt walked into the store. Six months ago if Nisha had seen this man at an airport she would not have placed him in the ranks of desirable customers, but she'd learned to recognize the softer expressions of luxury. This morning it was a monotone cap with the embroidered Gancini, from the wrist the burnished gleam of a

Richard Mille. A customer like this, she now knew, enjoyed the performance of equality, enjoyed having your respect though they'd be left uncomfortable by any hint of obsequiousness. Siddharth flashed a guilty smile over his shoulder, rushing forward though it was her turn.

Her first of the day, a young couple, arrived thirty minutes later. The man was in a crisp white shirt and the woman in a salwar kameez of simple elegance. The couple smiled politely but did not engage so Nisha backed away, smiling so they knew she was available. They wandered between the pedestal cases, perused the shelves along the rear wall. A few minutes later the man came up to her and coughed delicately.

'Hi ma'am. Could I have your assistance for just a minute?' he said. Late twenties, Nisha thought. From one of the office blocks down the road. The wife was wearing a Fitbit, but that could signify anything.

'How can I help?' Nisha asked.

He pointed to a shelf on the wall. 'I'm just trying to decide between these three. My boss, she's invited us to her home for dinner. I know she likes dark chocolate.'

Nisha placed them definitively now. Her mind flitted to an early conversation with Siddharth, the most lucrative advice she'd ever received: 'Most people are here to buy knowledge. Some facts they can keep in their minds to justify the expense. Always, people are hungry to learn. When someone comes in, you have to *teach* them how Dojuri is different.'

'One thing about dark chocolate,' Nisha said in a confidential tone, 'we tend to assume the darker the better. But actually, it's the opposite. Ordinary brands, high-street chocolate, it's usually *very* dark, almost black. That's because they over-roast the beans to get to the flavour. But quality dark chocolate is never black.'

The wife blinked a couple of times. 'I didn't know that,' she said.

'I didn't either, until I started working here,' Nisha said with a furtive, welcoming smile. She reached towards the register and selected one of the sample boxes they kept on the shelf underneath, removing the lid with both hands. 'Really good dark chocolate, you'll see a reddish tinge. Maroon-black, something like that.' She tapped along the name on the box she was holding. It wasn't the most expensive variety, but it would not shame them either. Smiled widely at the wife. 'I'm also a fan of dark chocolate, actually. This is my favourite. I'm sure she'll love it.'

They took two boxes, hesitating only briefly when she told them the price.

2

THE CORRIDORS WERE DIM AND the mall nearly empty. The new guy shut the glass doors, dropped the blinds, cut the overhead lights. Nisha wheeled in a midsize white screen from the backroom and soon a projector lit up a beam of floating mites. She had seen this slender Japanese lady three times now, talking in painstaking English about the excellence of the Dojuri brand. She waited for the admonitory tone: no compromises on quality or storage would be tolerated by Hokkaido. The spectre of liability hung darkly.

Watching the short training video reminded Nisha of her own first day. A prickle in her arms and legs as she ironed the uniform, zipped up the black skirt, adjusted her buttons so a modest triangle glowed at the throat; walking with purpose and confidence past the security and into the daunting lobby of Empirium Mall with its golden chandeliers and low honey lights and gliding aromas of lemongrass and green tea. The shop, too, was filled with a thick rich cocoa-butter smell. Sitting low in her plastic chair, Nisha sniffed the air, hoping to catch a whiff of the abundance that had suffused her senses that first day, when her manager Siddharth had used a long thumbnail to sever the shrink-wrap on a burnished copper box and lift the lid, revealing an umber slab of dusty chocolate unlike any she'd seen before, perfect cuts that hardly broke the surface, like chalk lines on a pavement. Siddharth looked up invitingly as the aroma wafted towards his nose, towards all their noses, giving them a warm smile, a welcome into this new world. Once their eyes were on him, Siddharth pushed down with a small wooden implement and broke off a few cubes, offering these to the two new employees, assuming an air of formality that struck Nisha strangely, that until then she'd associated with death. Then he folded the fine oily tissue over the remaining chocolate and returned the box to the counter. Nisha spent more than a minute with her cube, allowing it to drop from shape on to her tongue. She noted, when they were closing that evening, that Siddharth took the open box with him.

Nisha had this sudden sense of being trapped in her chair. The Japanese lady was using a pair of tongs to transfer cubes from a box to a large plate, her ivory white gloves smudged at the tips with cocoa dust. She fished out her phone to check the time, shielding the screen so the blue light would not distract the others. Even the world Nisha connected to online had started to feel the same. The usual fare for this time of evening: dancing, so much dancing, a new bend-and-pop had gone viral; pap footage of upcoming and outgoing actresses posing outside parties and gymnasiums; a selection of spaniels – she had a weakness for the breed; a group of attractive girls about her own age in aviator sunglasses and the distinctive shiny saris that young women wore to their graduation balls. Though she knew none of them she stepped through this online mirror that reflected the party, clicking upon the feeds of those who were tagged, finding different posts and more tags, the boys in overlarge suits, awkward curls to their facial hair, a beaten-down dance floor, girls swaying shoulder to shoulder, squinty eyes, bright ties, wide, accomplished smiles, the crushing finality of their romances.

She came to a smatter of posts from home. The forest fires were back, worse than ever it seemed. So many people she had gone to school with were posting horrifying pictures. A few of the same videos appeared on multiple accounts. Hillsides alight, long curving lines of conifers on fire, a soundtrack of deep throaty crackling. Suddenly she longed for the bracing damp air that would hit her cheeks as she stepped on to the path behind her home that they used as a shortcut to the upper reaches of the town, the trees closing in until it began to feel like a tunnel through the forest, the fecund smells and gentle, mysterious buzzing, ahead of her the steady tramp of her sister or father. Now life was inside an air-conditioned mall. A ballerina in a snow globe. She returned to the video, nudging the thought away. Her father had stories of fighting the fires two decades ago, when they had three torrid summers in succession, going out on night patrol with his lepidopterist boss. This summer was peculiar, Baba said. There had been rain. And the heat had long let up. Still in October these fires raged. Funny also, she felt, that you hardly heard of the forest fires in Delhi. Six hours away, a straight shot down the Moradabad highway, an hour's climb once you were past Haldwani, yet when she was in the city all that felt like a different world. The city created its own urgencies and each one, it seemed, drew her away from home. Here in Delhi she had to summon that sense of loss, force herself to remember the forests, to think her way back to mornings and afternoons spent in dark green bowers. The Tripathi boys and Shiva had been posting the most. They went out night after night to beat back the flames and drink.

She felt sharply annoyed at being made to sit through this training video again. Her toes drew up involuntarily, curling against the roof of her mules. It helped, feeling her own exasperation. She would've got up and left if it weren't for Siddharth. He liked to impress the owner, Mrs Jain, by making them stay late occasionally for things like this. The film ended, the lights came on. Deven, the new recruit, seemed startled by the deluge of instruction. Nisha stretched, twisting to either side in her chair. Siddharth looked at her, then down at his watch. 'I'm off,' he said brightly, his narrow face crinkling into a smile. So she was to show Deven how to close the store.

Once they'd cleaned, emptied the trash, locked up, Deven gestured to move to the escalators together, but she told him to go ahead. She waited outside the store, freshening her make-up using the camera of her phone, until he had been deposited safely on the ground floor. Then she walked the long way around the circular balcony, her heels loud now that the halls were empty. Only the restaurants were still going, semi-dark, filled with fabulous heedless people bearing wine-purple lips, stuck in each other's eyes behind their plate-glass aquarium windows. As soon as she stepped outside Nisha felt happy.

Low over the manmade hillock hung a near full moon, like a scoop of butterscotch that had lightly been licked. Siddharth was deeply interested in her past. This made her happy. He envied especially the recollections she shared when they'd just made love. She told him of walks with her sister and cousins around the lakes, on narrow paths that ATVs had now taken over: honeymoon couples rented them for half an hour but promptly got stuck, unable to turn around, so a local boy would run after them, ready to take over from the sheepish groom. Sliding along the pine-needle slopes collecting cones. Ludo by candlelight to while away the load-shedding evenings. He loved the story of the abandoned house a hundred feet above their home that was haunted by an Englishman. Snakes in the lake. That afternoon they were swimming by the long bank at Naukuchiatal and a dead man floated by.

Finally an autorickshaw muttered to a halt at her feet. She boarded, thinking how thrilling it was to be with someone like Siddharth. He knew so much, was so very good at his job. Back home the girls were being cajoled into marriage, usually with some clueless boy. Siddharth was a man. More – a gentleman. If she was honest, this relationship, this city boy, more even than her job, gave her a sense of being better than the life she'd left behind. Didn't some girls say that about her in school, that she thought she was better than everyone? But she never behaved that way. A lot of that was jealousy. It happened if you were a bit prettier.

A small and crowded pizza place in Basant Lok market that she could not really afford but hoped

Siddharth would like, or, more candidly, be impressed by. He would joke sometimes, say if she made a comment while they were watching a film, or if she was confused by an option on a delivery app, that she was a small-town girl at heart. She did not properly understand why he made her nervous, she who had always felt confident. He had a sense of himself that she envied. He could talk to anyone. He even got along so well with the owner, Mrs Jain, whenever she came into the shop. And as they talked and joked it seemed they both knew he was destined for more than the shop. It was because of Mrs Jain that they had to keep their relationship secret. Why they would never leave work together.

The glass door to the pizza place dinged open into a different world, filled with the kind of aunties, uncles and malcontent children who might buy Dojuri on a whim while walking through the mall completing their real shopping. There was a thick smell of singed flour, a giant red dog decal, Coldplay on the stereo. At first she couldn't find him. Then she saw that reassuring grin. Siddharth was waving at her from a two-seater on the upper level. She smiled thinly in return. As she walked up the steps, one thought beat in her mind: Should she tell him?

He was on his feet as she approached, pulling out a chair. She leaned in, caressed his shoulder, gave him a peck with a slight sense of embarrassment. Siddharth wanted to know how the new boy closed, and at first the talk remained of work. It was only as their enormous slices arrived, dangling cheese and dripping grease, that Siddharth put his foot against hers underneath the table. She slid her toes back and forth along his shin, enjoying the feel of him tensing up in excitement, the catch in his voice as he attempted to continue the conversation. She looked at the time on her phone. Mrs Ahluwalia, the owner and operator of her PG, was expecting her back by 11.30.

'You know my friend Allana, at Bottega?' Nisha said.

'Of course,' Siddharth said. 'Nice girl.'

Nisha looked up in surprise. 'I didn't know you guys talked.' She smiled to hide whatever it was she'd briefly felt. 'Allana told me the funniest story today. About one of their regulars. This old guy. Usually dressed in a suit, nice shirt. Speaks really well. They Googled him. Industrialist.'

'See, that's what we don't get at Dojuri,' Siddharth said with a slight frown. 'Those top top guys. Probably we get their wives. Or their assistants. Not the men themselves. One day that's going to be me. Just you see.'

Nisha flinched, almost unnoticeably. Siddharth's various futures never comprised a 'we'. She admonished herself for being needy, even clingy. She had to abandon that small-town mindset. These were the experiences she'd travelled all this way for.

'So, this guy,' Nisha went on, 'he does this strange thing every time he comes to the store. Which is very often. He'll choose one of their fanciest handbags. But he won't buy one. He'll buy two. One he'll pay with his credit card, and one he'll pay cash.'

'Too much black money?'

'That's what they thought. Anyway, most of their customers like to buy in cash. They're used to that. So the manager, he told this guy, sir, please don't worry, don't carry so much cash in. Their bags go for two, two and half lakhs. I'll send the bags to your house and you can hand over the payment there.' She sprinkled chilli flakes on her slice, smiling mischievously. 'This guy, though, this big, powerful industrialist, suddenly he looked scared. He said, no, no, don't ever send it to my house. One of these is for my wife. The other is for … That's why I buy two of the same thing. Dress, diamond, whatever it is. So I don't get confused about what I've given each one. I just give them the same thing.'

Siddharth laughed, leaning back in his chair. 'That's great. That's power. Real power.'

'Power? He's frightened of his wife! She checks his credit card statement.'

'Yeah, because she'll take all that he's worked so hard for. But he manages. Does what he needs. And see – even one bag is out of reach for ninety-nine per cent of the world. He buys two like it's nothing. That's power,' he repeated ruefully. 'I just need to make it to the head office. Once I'm there…' He suddenly looked around, as if he'd remembered that life waited for no one. 'Ice cream?' he asked. 'Or should we go?'

Nisha swallowed, nodding. She had been hoping to go to Nirula's, a short walk across the small, disused fountain, for dessert. They could have the chat in a new place, maybe enjoy a sundae. But she could tell he wanted to get going. Siddharth could slip into a barbed manner when things weren't just as he'd planned. She took a tissue from the table and carefully wiped the grease from her fingers and mouth, building her nerve.

'There's something I have to tell you,' Nisha said.

Siddharth looked up from his plate, one eyebrow cresting. 'About what?'

Suddenly her courage failed. It was too early, she told herself, what, three days? As usual she was being fretful beyond need. Her cycle could easily have matched with Shobita's. That happens to flatmates sometimes, she'd read. It occurred to her that this might not be the first time a girl had brought up something like this with Siddharth. She looked into his eyes but could not picture a reaction.

'I just … just need to stop by the chemist on the way,' she said.

'What do you need?' Siddharth said, chewing the last of his slice.

'Just some girly stuff,' she smiled. 'You don't get to peek.'

Siddharth looked up at the ceiling, lips pursed like a smoker, absently patting his obliques with a worried expression as if the pizza had already made its way there. Nisha exhaled slowly. But they didn't go for ice cream to Nirula's, or even order dessert at the restaurant. She did notice, as she paid the bill, in the aisle under the bright white lights at the chemist's, as they climbed into his father's WagonR and began the drive to their favourite spot, that Siddharth would shoot her furtive glances, a strange, distant expression on his face, like he was trying to figure something out but it kept slipping from his hands.

By the time they turned off the main Ghitorni road on to the little lane with its optimistic name – even during the day, there was little greenery to be seen – found the cul de sac and parked by the power transformer, Siddharth seemed to have wiped the matter from his mind. His hand went to the lever by his side, and his seat jerked back a few degrees. He smiled at her and patted his thigh. Nisha's brain and body tingled with anticipation, but she shook her head demurely, happy to have control, knowing he was happy to be for once acquiescent. She played pointed fingernails in the soft hairs of his nape, delicately incising, enjoyed their parallel excitement. The road was empty, dark save the moonlight catching the curling barbed wire atop the farmhouse walls on either side, the strewn packets of blue and white polythene that formed a kind of pavement. He leaned across and began to nuzzle her neck. Eventually she hiked her skirt up and shifted her underwear and slid down upon him, her arms around his neck, Siddharth almost animal now in his kneading and gnawing, and as she worked with her bare knees pushing down on to the damp faux-wool of the front seat she reared back so she could look upon him and she could see what he wanted of her, she had always seen, she could see even how long he would want it but it did not matter for she could take too, it did not matter for she could see in his half-lidded eyes that she was beautiful, powerful, loved.

3

NISHA KNEW IMMEDIATELY WHERE HER sister was sitting. Under one of the squared white umbrellas in the garden of the cafe that had opened a few years ago on the Bhowali road. Over Rupa's shoulder, beneath a white-and-blue sky, Nisha could see familiar strings of outsize naked bulbs, unlit at this time, though as the sun began to set they would diffuse a warm amber light upon the grass. It was still early enough that Rupa would have had to swipe the thick layer of dew from the wrought iron chair she sat on, from the table where she'd placed her laptop. Nisha felt a sharp twinge as she caught a glimpse of home.

When was the last time she'd been up? May, for her sister's wedding. Simple ceremony. A temple in the clouds, chosen by their mother, built into the side of the summit, the structure divided into three segments linked by a rising corridor of broad stone steps. Nisha smiled as she thought about her mother that day. She looked beautiful in a forest-green Kanjeevaram embellished with zari motifs. But rockslides had turned the road tenuous. The ancient family Alto would sometimes slide shakily to the brink as they took a turn, and because the narrow broken path wound in vicious reiteration around this high peak her mother began to feel sick, shouting at Nisha's father until he rattled to a halt so she could lean out the door, draw back her hair, hurl out breakfast.

'You've been seeing Mumma-Papa?' Nisha asked.

'I try to spend one night a week at home. Papa is over the moon right now. Havicek called him up and said, I need you, something happened to the collection, something they'd dealt with a long time ago, weevils or something. They were eating the wings. Papa is so proud to be called in at his age.'

'I think he misses those butterflies more than he misses me,' Nisha said. They both laughed. 'And how's my bhinju? Keeping you happy?'

'Really happy,' Rupa said with a shy smile. In school Rupa excelled at art, cracked a competitive exam, studied design in Ahmedabad. Afterwards, instead of going to Delhi or Mumbai she had returned, working with local textile artists, though she paid her bills by conceiving designs and branding for the great glut of hotels, play zones, camping sites and bed and breakfasts that were opening up all over their hills. Through this all Rupa had remained seemingly unattached. Nisha had never understood why. Then she met Manoj, a journalist for Nainital's chief newspaper, through their cousin Umesh. He was perhaps six inches taller than her, with dark mottled cheeks and a smiling demeanour. 'What about you? When are you bringing Siddharth up?'

'Never!' Nisha smiled, a little thinly. She did not want to mention that Siddharth had been behaving somewhat strange with her since that dinner three nights ago. She did not want to mention her period had still not come. She missed the closeness of their childhood, before her sister went away. 'I wouldn't embarrass Papa-Mumma like that.' Regret, as those words emerged, for Nisha saw her older sister's face fall.

'Like I did?' she said, her cheeks drawn, teeth tight.

'Stop that, that's not what I meant,' Nisha said.

But she could not help thinking back to the day of the wedding. It must have been mid-morning by the time Nisha escaped with her father from the smoky, overheated chamber where the ceremony was taking place, settling on the cool stone parapet just outside so they could be summoned as needed. A glacial crosswind scampered across the complex, the parapets on either side yielding to tree-lined mountains as a thick mist wrapped around the tessellated shikharas like the white chiffon of a sari. Cousins, aunts and uncles had arrived from all over the region, some travelling from as far as upper Garhwal on a brutal bus journey. Everyone looked bright, happy, polished by the strong morning sun.

Her cousin Umesh ducked out of the room, spotting them, and came up with a grin. 'Too hot, too hot.' He took off the smart black pahadi hat that he always wore now – Rupa said it was a signal of his rising political ambition – and wiped his hairline with a handkerchief. 'I guess we have to go all the way down for a cigarette?' He sat down heavily beside Nisha.

'So, Bade Papa, happy today?' he continued. 'Must be a relief it's finally happening. Two days, then you can relax.' He pointed to Nisha. 'Until this one's ready. I don't know how you live in that filthy city. It's so hot there all the time.'

'I like it,' Nisha said, a touch defensively.

'At least you must be earning well,' Umesh said. 'Here there's nothing. Only if you have land you have money.' He took out a cigarette and began to tap the filter on the small dark gold packet. He nodded at the chamber in which the marriage ceremony was taking place. 'You know earlier what they used to do, na, when a girl married outside their caste. Any land she was going to inherit would go to the brother, or a cousin.' He laughed. 'I'm right here if you want to give.'

'Bhaiya!' Nisha said. 'That's *your* friend!'

'Of course. He's good fun to drink with. Plays teen patti. But who asked your sister to marry him? Only Rupa would do some mad thing like this.'

That morning her father had not responded to Umesh's provocation, save a gentle mumble about his daughter's choice, which had made Nisha wonder what he really thought. She had told herself that her father was a man of science and study, mild in his ways, spending most of his life assisting an accomplished local lepidopterist with the upkeep of his collection, more interested, now, in their small garden than anything else. Why should he care what his wolf of a nephew had to say? But she could not help wonder what would happen if she were to bring Siddharth up to their home, as Rupa suggested. How would they all react?

She focused on the screen – her sister had the look of recounting something important.

'... he just got a big break at work. You've been seeing about the fires? It's really bad Ranikhet side. Even Almora.'

'I saw,' Nisha said. 'Those videos look crazy.'

'So, the editor decided to send Manoj. Try and find out what's going on. Why they're happening so late in the year. On TV they were saying it might be because of climate change. He'll travel to those tiny villages around there. Talk to the villagers.'

'Last time I came up he was complaining about only writing stories about the parking issues on Mall Road,' Nisha smiled. 'He must be very excited.'

4

'PALLADIUM IS KILLING US,' SAID Siddharth. 'All month. What are we going to do about it?'

Nisha tried to focus. It was the quiet afternoon hour, when all the city seemed to drowse, so Siddharth had squeezed in an informal meeting of 'his' crew. She knew Palladium by name of course, the ultra-luxury mall in Mumbai that housed the first flagship outlet. This was what scared her, a little, about technology. The cloud-based POS system installed by the owners some months ago now put the sales data for each outlet into a central system. It was intended to facilitate inventory management and various flows, but Nisha hadn't noticed much of a change. Instead she observed that Siddharth was becoming preoccupied with the sales the other outlets were managing – Bangalore, Calcutta, Lucknow, of course Mumbai. Every morning, he would check each city's leading outlet and grumble or gloat.

But today Siddharth wasn't stressed. He turned away from Deven so only Nisha could see his face, narrowing his eyes into a cheeky half-smile. She grinned back. Things had been so weird between them. Yet their relationship seemed to have turned a corner. All this morning he'd been warm, courteous, playful. He'd even caressed the top of her hand once, when he was sure no one could see, making the backs of her knees tingle with pleasure. It was puzzling, to say the least. He seemed to have forgiven her. Nisha wasn't sure exactly what she was being forgiven for but she felt grateful all the same. Perhaps that wasn't the right word. Relieved. It was relief that rippled through her all that day, ever since she'd received that open, hospitable smile just as she walked in.

Siddharth straightened his features, resumed his official bearing. 'As you both know, we're also at the end of the month,' he said. 'There's some stock from last month's orders that is nearing expiry. I placed those orders, so I'm directly responsible if we fail to fulfil. Any ideas how to dispose?'

'Offer a discount?' Deven said.

'That's against policy. Dilutes the brand,' Siddharth said impatiently.

'We could do an early Diwali display,' Nisha said, lightly scratching the mole on the crest of her left cheekbone, an old tic that usually meant she was thinking. 'Something for the front of the store.'

'Not a bad idea, Nisha. Good memory,' Siddharth slowly said. She felt a rush of pride. 'We're not quite at the festival, of course, but it's worth trying. Let's do it.' Again he shot her a mysterious look. Then he turned to Deven. 'You don't need to worry about closing today. Nisha and I will take care of it. You've been working hard. You can leave a little early.'

In the late afternoon, as Siddharth handled the customers, Nisha and Deven fashioned an impressive pyramidal structure out of three dozen Dojuri boxes, the scumbled-copper insignia on the lids shining sombre under the arc lights. Good enough to see from the moon, Nisha joked, but neither boy seemed to get it. All that afternoon as she stacked and finessed the placement of each box Nisha's heart hummed with a secret pleasure. In the time they'd worked together Siddharth and she had never closed the store alone. He was too careful; it would never be just the two of them. The dimmed corridors at closing time, dark staircases, hidden cubby-like rooms, the cavernous parking lot. She had to control herself before her body and mind became too heated. This must be Siddharth's way of overcoming the distance that had come between them during this miserable week. He had missed her touch the way she wanted his. All day she had been catching whiffs of his scent, the special cologne he wore on his neck when they went out. It was driving her to distraction.

The last customer was a dawdler. Nisha knew her well. Dolly something. A girthy woman, always smiling evilly through her thick, lightly smudged lipstick. This evening she inspected the wares with maddening care, though the range hardly ever changed, and Nisha caught herself willing the lady out of the store, mentally grabbing her by the shoulder and escorting her out like a bouncer at a bar.

'What's so funny?' Siddharth whispered, coming around from behind her.

'Oh, sorry,' Nisha said, and had to look down to the carpet to avoid flushing with embarrassment. She leaned in close, trying to invest her words with meaning. 'Just looking forward to closing.'

A strange look, as if of fear, flashed across Siddharth's face. Then he was back to normal. He wandered to Dolly, but returned a couple of minutes later, standing in front of her and taking a deep breath. 'Listen, there's something I've been meaning to tell you,' he said. 'A month ago, I put in an application for a position at the head office. Mrs Jain said I should. It's a big opportunity. Real chance for me.'

Overcome by surprise, Nisha blinked a few times, and later, when she played the moment over, she felt sure she must've looked stupid, gaping wordless like that. She couldn't understand at first how it hadn't come up before. It seemed in that moment like she didn't really recognize this man who was speaking to her. The face was oddly unfamiliar. Before she could say anything, however, Siddharth said 'oh god' and departed once again, this time for the checkout counter, where Deven was struggling with Dolly's purchases. He smiled reassuringly at the older woman, smoothly slotting in as Deven retreated into the recess. Suddenly, without apparent reason, Nisha remembered the only tattoo Siddharth had on his body. It was quite large, taking up one half of his upper chest. She had placed her head on his stomach and touched each line with a fingertip. A beautifully shaded fig tree with heart-shaped leaves, the Bodhi tree, Siddharth had explained, and just underneath, in stylized cursive, the words 'Seeking Enlightenment'. Nisha had been so impressed by that. Not only the reference to the man he was named after, the god, one should say, Nisha had been impressed because boys her age liked to claim so many things about themselves, I'm this, I'm that, look at me, and here was this guy, just a few years older, this sophisticated man, still searching, who knew he was still searching.

Once Dolly had departed, Siddharth ushered Deven out, and only then returned to her. His smile was a little less sure now.

'Isn't the head office in Mumbai?' Nisha asked. It felt like her stomach was in the basement of the building, in the parking lot somewhere.

'Yeah, it is. But I haven't got the job yet,' Siddharth said.

'Oh! Okay,' Nisha said. She did not want to hold him back, but she didn't want the alternative either.

'I mean, they've told me informally. I got the call this morning. The offer letter has to come still.'

'I see,' Nisha said.

'I'll be training at the Delhi office for two months. It's not like we have to stop right away,' Siddharth said. 'But only if we keep it really quiet. I can't take a chance now. You understand.'

Nisha nodded. She walked to the nook and turned off the music. Immediately she was glad for the absence of the downtempo electronica, which felt, all of a sudden, like the aural backdrop to her life, to her ambitions and future.

'It's just…' Siddharth said, following her, 'I've been feeling weird about us in any case. And then this job news.'

Nisha nodded again. But she didn't say anything. What a word, weird, how much weight it could carry. Siddharth sounded different too. She realized it had been happening for a while. Earlier, as it issued instructions at work, his voice had played in her head with the swift, calming reassurance of a mountain stream, but now it sounded a bit conscious, a bit strained, as if determined to be impersonal, a metallic monotone no different and no more real than the announcer's on the metro.

5

6:23 PM Hey...
6:23 PM How's it going
6:23 PM Did you reply to him?

7:03 PM Not yet
7:04 PM Can't think what to say. Feeling a little sick last few days

7:10 PM How are you managing at work? Isn't it difficult, him hovering about?
7:10 PM Been thinking about you a lot
7:11 PM You should try to come home for a bit

9:34 PM Just got home
9:34 PM Can't right now

Mother India

> 9:34 PM Imagine applying for leave
> 9:35 PM His ego will explode
> 9:35 PM As it is I catch him looking at me sometimes. He looks so sure of everything
> 9:36 PM Like he can see what he's done and it gives a sense of pride
> 9:36 PM You haven't said anything to Mumma Papa have you?

9:40 PM Am I mad?
9:41 PM Not without asking you

> 9:42 PM Oh ok
> 9:42 PM Got a strange message from Ma

9:48 PM Told her you weren't feeling great
9:48 PM That you've been having some work stuff

> 10:31 PM Ok
> 10:31 PM Will talk to her tomorrow
> 10:31 PM Not that there's anything to say

10:53 PM Just take it easy

10:53 PM It won't matter in a few weeks

10:55 PM It won't matter as much

11:01 PM Yeah

11:01 PM There was something else, actually

11:01 PM We were kind of fighting

11:03 PM OYE

11:08 PM What is this???

11:09 PM What happened?

11:09 PM What is what?

11:10 PM So weird

11:10 PM Manoj is out on assignment you know. He's gone to Ranikhet for that forest fire story

11:10 PM Half a mountainside gone

11:10 PM But he just sent me the strangest forward

11:11 PM So you know that Kumaoni Whatsapp group I showed you? The one that Umesh bhaiya mods. All day the group has been blowing up. I don't even notice any more. Muted it long time ago

11:11 PM But Nishoo, today they were all really angry about something. Maybe not all. Just a few is enough.

Mother India

But they were posting and posting. It seemed to be about that student union guy in Delhi. Did you read about him?

11:12 PM I'm so confused

11:12 PM No idea

11:13 PM Oh maybe I did see something. They arrested him?

11:13 PM Someone screenshotted some tweets

11:17 PM He's the guy who caused a big fuss cos he won't say Bharat Mata ki jai

11:17 PM It was all over the TV news. The channel up here went crazy. They were saying send a police team from Nainital to arrest him

11:18 PM Ok...

11:19 PM But this is the strange bit ... why I'm telling you now. I'm staring at it and staring at it

11:19 PM What is it?

11:19 PM It's you, Nishoo. That's what I can't understand

THREE

1

'BALDIE *SAID* HE'D PAY US extra if she went viral,' Sushil said. He spat into the dust at their feet, then took another sip. 'Nothing.'

In front of Mayank and Sushil sat two plastic bottles. One, labelled 'Union Jack Whisky', was half full with a golden-brown liquid. A litre bottle of Pepsi had also been procured to cut the unique Union burn. They sat on the pavement under the flyover that humped over the intersection of the Mahipalpur–Mehrauli road. The mood, the night, the light, all were irate. Mayank grunted in response.

'Proper viral,' Sushil muttered. 'Everyone saw it.'

'I get this bad feeling in my stomach when I think about it,' Mayank said. He paused, twisting his neck as a soft whine arrowed towards them, echoing upon the ramparts overhead, growing into a growl, an enormous sound that folded around the pillars and rained down from the concrete beams and cross-girders. They waited in silence, with a sense of both awe and disgust, as a white Audi R8 approached the intersection. The windows were tinted into mirrors but Mayank imagined low-slung seats, black leather, a young couple. The Audi took a careful left, roaring as it burst away. For a few seconds they basked in the fresh onset of silence. The liquor was making Mayank's head spin. Perhaps talking would help. 'I wish we'd had more time.'

'Time for what?' Sushil asked.

'Remember where we got the face?'

Sushil thought about this. 'Someone's feed, right?'

'Kashyap was in such a hurry to get it out. To beat everyone else. We didn't have time to make adjustments. That AI rendered the face using just her photos.'

'How does it matter? Even if she sees it, she'll never guess,' Sushil laughed. 'And even if she guesses, she'll never know it was us.'

I check her feed every day, Mayank almost said. I think I love her. He realized how maudlin and weak the alcohol had made him.

'Only you could find the shit in a field of dreams,' Sushil went on. 'Wasn't it amazing, going viral like that? That was our work. Kashyap says so himself. That's the feeling I want again.'

'Easy to say. How to do?'

An enigmatic smile took over Sushil's face. 'Well, my friend,' he said, 'I've brought you to the place.'

'Here?' Mayank looked around in surprise. On either side pale street lights stretched into the night. Occasional scooters puttered up the flyover, cars preened past, but the apartment blocks were dark, shadowed and forbidding. All about seemed emptiness.

Sushil nodded his head southwards. 'You know what's down the road, don't you?'

'The metro station?'

'Brother, why would we film a metro station? We're going to the Bengali basti.'

'The slum?'

'Where the Bangladeshis are. They call it Jai Hind Camp. That doesn't fool me.'

Mayank felt off-balance. Things had sped up. All of a sudden he could see himself sitting down there in the ferric dust, mind afloat, trapped inside a moment both alien and intimate. 'When our ancestors ruled this area,' he said finally, 'exactly one thousand years ago, they built forts that still stand today. Reservoirs. Tanks. All the way to Surajkund. That huge lake is built by them. Just imagine that.' He looked around the dark street, then up at the concrete grey underside of the flyover. 'Will anything we make today last a thousand years?'

'Bhai you love to talk this history talk, don't you?' Sushil said. 'Where do you get this stuff?'

'Facebook,' Mayank shrugged. 'Internet. There's a website dedicated to our history. The guy, the website owner, he's your gotra, actually. Tokas. I wrote an email to him the other day. Lives in the UK. Runs it from there all by himself.'

Sushil poured a hefty measure into both their glasses, recapped the bottle, and placed it on the road. Mayank sloshed in some Pepsi. Warm bubbles rose up his oesophagus.

'They built the first layer of this city,' Mayank said, pride beginning to beat in his blood. He pointed in the direction the Audi had come from. 'Down there, my village, named after Mahipal, one of the first kings of Delhi.' He pointed down the road the Audi had selected. 'And your village, Munirka. Tokas ruled since 1400. This all used to be yours. Vasant Kunj, R.K. Puram. Government acquired it after Independence. Even the university where Student of the Year is studying today.'

'You think I don't know?' Sushil said in a bored voice. 'I've heard these stories since I was a baby. Who cares? What difference does it make when we're sitting on the side of the road?'

'I feel happy when I read these things. Doesn't it make you feel happy?' Mayank stood up. 'Come on, if we're going, let's go. We'll drink and walk.'

Sushil stretched lazily, then rose himself. 'Okay, let me tell you a story now. A story you won't ever read in a history book. About my clan. Nowadays we do boxing, wrestling, all that. But did you know we're the best swimmers in the whole country?'

'Swimmers? Here?' Mayank flung his arm out, as if to remind his friend of the forlorn buildings, the spare shivering trees and desert air. 'What are you talking about?'

'After Independence, most of the swimmers were Tokas, you know. Olympics, Asian Games, National Games. They all used to come from this village. There was a special lake here. A baba from Ayodhya had blessed it. He said, as long as there is water in this lake, amazing swimmers will come from here. And it was true. There was even a gold medallist from our village. But then construction started. Ring Road, all the colonies that side. The lake dried up. Government told our swimmers to start practising in a pool. My grandfather was one of the men who took a petition to the government, explaining we need the water from the lake, the lake is what gives us our strength.' Sushil drained his blue plastic glass, spinning around like a shot-putter so he could hurl it high into the dark night. He grunted from the sudden exertion. 'It hasn't been the same since. Ever since they made us start swimming in a pool. Not one more medal.'

*

The boys overshot the Jai Hind Camp of probable infiltrates by some distance, only breaking their springy sozzled stride when the headlights of a truck blaring its horn landed upon their backs, the driver's assistant leaning out of his window to protest via an unyielding yell this pair of goat-brained miscreants who walked in the middle of the road at night. This sobered them up somewhat. Just as they got their bearings they spotted the sign for the camp. Adjacent to it was a small triangular park which they began to walk towards, noticing a line of cycle rickshaws that buttressed one wall, metal frames gleaming under the street light, the bulb horns ornamented with rainbow-feathered tresses. Each of the rickshaws was occupied, its operator slumbering upon the raised blue seat with his legs and arms dangling off.

'Look at them,' Sushil said. 'Coming to our country for a better life.'

The night was still as a stone and even from this distance Mayank could see fat mosquitoes hovering over the sleeping bodies, locating landing strips, drawing murderous, futile slaps in response. 'I wonder if they'll find it,' Mayank said.

Sushil gave him a curious gaze. 'Government will sort them out. You need a strong man to deal with such people.' He hopped on to the parapet, throwing a theatrical leg over the spoked fence, tumbling briefly as he descended to the other side. Mayank followed in more circumspect fashion. He looked around with mild wonder, for he had hardly ever been out this late, certainly never while so flagrantly buzzed, and everything his eye caught seemed to throb with mystery: the black, unmoving outlines of the trees, the battered swing set, the rough hedge that carried along the perimeter and looked suddenly like a magician's beard.

'Still recording?' he whispered.

Sushil started, suddenly remembering, and looked down into his shirt pocket, adjusting the phone that was in it so that the lens of the camera could once again see. He touched the tips of his thumb and forefinger, resting them on his lower lip, and bit down gently, letting out a piercing whistle that sent the birds bursting from the trees and started a chain of barks from the mongrels of the area.

'Where is everyone? Usually, one of the guys is out here at least. You think it's too late?'

A question occurred to Mayank. 'How many times have you come here before?'

Suddenly a dark head poked up from behind the wall. 'What?' it asked.

'Weed,' said Sushil. 'No, smack. Get smack.'

The head laughed, then disappeared. A huge bird returned noiselessly to the park canopy. The voice appeared again right behind the duo, making them jump. They spun around to see a short man in a sleeveless white undershirt and lungi. 'You know what time it is?' he asked. He took a closer look at them. 'What do you two boys want with such a thing anyway?'

'Who are you calling a boy?' Sushil said, taking his voice down a couple of notches.

Mayank began to worry about how he would come across, in comparison, in the viral video. 'Yeah, who are you calling a boy?' he said, and took a threatening step forward.

The small man raised his hands in peace. 'Relax, relax. I didn't mean anything. It's just, that's not a good thing. Let me get you some weed. You boys ... sorry, you men ... you don't want that.'

'Who are you, Mahatma Gandhi?' Sushil said.

The man assumed an expression of doubt. 'I can ask around. But it's so late, sir. Don't really know if…'

'Get some smack or I'll give you a tight one,' Sushil said.

Mayank felt once again a prickle of uncertainty about the impression he and his partner would leave on the viewers of the viral video. 'Weed is fine too,' he intervened. 'Get us some weed. How much are you charging?'

Sushil swivelled around in surprise, then thought for a couple of seconds. The man flashed a toothy white smile and disappeared. 'You keep turning to look at me, donkey,' Mayank said. 'Don't get my face on camera. We'll have to edit it out.'

Suddenly they heard a yelp. The boys looked at each other, alarmed, and then in the direction of the departed dealer, from where came the sound of pounding feet, a pursuit. Mayank squinted, struggling as he was to pick out anything, when the curtained darkness was parted by a sudden blaze. A huge flashlight played upon the tin walls of the camp, irradiating the recent clouds of yellow dust. In the penumbral light Mayank could see two policemen moving swiftly in the direction of the gate, swinging the powerful beam here and there but failing to pick out the man they'd seen. It was Mayank who then failed to realize that the constables were turning their light and gaze towards the park, so Sushil grabbed his shoulder and just in time pulled him down to the ground. They flattened themselves on their backs, legs stretched, necks against the wall so nothing of their heads would be seen. The light danced just above their heads now, scanning the breadth of the park. A warm sweat bathed Mayank's pits and dripped from his nape on to the earth. As the torch beam probed the dust overhead Mayank began a quick prayer, asking for forgiveness, leeway, his mother, anything that might extract him from this place. The constables began to argue over the best course to pursue.

Eyes still shut, Mayank counted slowly to fifty. When he opened them once again he was delighted to see the light had disappeared. As he craned his neck and looked around, he noted that Sushil had disappeared too. Mayank silently cursed his colleague. Scuffed prints in the dust indicated that Sushil had crawled to the other end of the park, jumping over the wall to his escape at the same spot where they'd entered a few minutes ago. Carefully, slowly, Mayank poked his head over the parapet. There was nobody to be seen. The constables were gone, the dealer disappeared into the camp, presumably not to return. Still Mayank found he was frozen by fear. Each time he tried to move, his legs and arms failed to comply. He was lying on his back, wondering what he could do, when he remembered the steady weight against his chest. The plastic bottle of Union Jack. A half of gold-brown courage still left within. He sat up, put the opening to his lips, drank until he could not, enjoying the heat push its way in, give life to his limbs. After a few minutes of steady swigging the bottle was almost empty and Mayank felt great. He stood suddenly, a touch unsteadily, then made his way elegantly – no crawl or crouch for him – to the other end of the park, where the rickshaw drivers still slept. These were not the effluent hours: the city breathed freely, the air smelt brighter, lighter, a hint of mulberry creeping from the bushes along the boundary wall.

He studied the sleepers for signs of migrant venality; but it is hard to tell if someone is illegal as they sleep, they issue the same sounds and the legs twitch still to the primal simian beat. Mayank was feeling tremendous now, almost affectionate towards these men. He unscrewed the bottle cap, took the long final sip, and tossed the bottle into a bush. An ethanol wave crashed into him, making the sky teeter in a slow, methodical manner. Hopping on to the parapet, he threw his left leg over the fence, clutching tight to keep from swaying, and he was about to shift over when a broad bright light swung on to his person.

Mayank froze. He took one hand off the fence and sat upright, deep in fright. All he could see was a pair of blinding beacons, around them a deep blackness, and if he heard any sounds in his panic he did not register them. His mind played a reel of what the police constables were seeing: Mayank perched between the spear-like spokes of this park fence, muddied, fuddled, one leg on either side, he could see himself as clearly as he could see the rickshaw drivers who'd been sleeping on the seats of their vehicles because they had jumped up now and were scattering in something like slow motion, their shouts and pleading distant, soft, and perhaps because he was frozen in this odd way at this small height from their scurrying about he felt for a moment like a king at battle astride a gallant steed, smiling at the madness he'd suddenly dropped into, this one-sided war, he felt enlarged by the sense that he was hovering outside himself and he did not even notice he'd started to sway, back and forth in gathering speed so when he keeled over completely it felt like it had happened all of a sudden, a drop in stylish, splendid abandon on to the pavement along the park.

*

When he woke his cheek hurt. A sharp ache shot immediately into his jaw, along his neck and shoulders.

He found he was in the back of a blue police van along with a half-dozen rickshaw drivers. The van was familiar from hundreds of movies but he'd never seen the inside of one, with its rough facing benches and the small caged window beyond which the night-time city rolled by, uncaring of his new plight. Mayank sat well apart from the rickshaw drivers, who were babbling in Bhojpuri or Bengali – he could not tell which and did not care to find out.

The van went along a bumpy road alongside a market and took a sharp turn into a compound. There was a kind of clamour outside. Jostling, shouting, for a few seconds the van rocked like a boat. The driver laid into the horn, the constable in the front seat climbed out and began to shout, 'Fall back, fall back, everybody fall back. He's inside, assholes. This is not him. He's already inside. Fall! Back!' The rocking slowed and then stopped altogether. The din ebbed. For a few minutes there was complete peace inside and out of the van.

Presently the double doors were drawn open by a large constable. A cold wind swirled freshly amid the sweaty fetor that had occupied the air inside. The rickshaw drivers filed out, looking at the ground. Mayank followed, still keeping his distance. When he hopped down on to the ground he turned to the constable with a friendly smile and raised a finger, saying, 'My friend, I think there's been some sort of mistake.'

'I'm not your friend,' the constable explained, after his robust palm found the cheek Mayank had planted upon in his plummet from the fence. The contact was a matter in Mayank's ears for some minutes. He allowed himself to be ushered without further objection into a police station with yellow walls and low ceilings and then past the painted metal bars of a cell. He was surprised to find they'd placed him in the same cell as the rickshaw drivers – poor chaps were still confused – but he found himself without opportunity to address this with anyone who mattered. He lay silently in a corner, nursing the pain and cursing his luck. Within minutes he fell into a desultory sleep.

2

MAYANK WALKED WITH THE RICKSHAW drivers in single file down a corridor, making soft circuitous pleas to the policeman, explaining that he'd lived in Delhi all his life, couldn't they tell, either line dating hundreds of years on this soil. The uniform told him what would happen if he didn't sober up. They entered a dark, windowless room that smelled like the puddles in a train-station latrine. Mayank decided he had to be brave. He walked up to the constable and said, 'I have all my paperwork. Just let me go home to get it. Government ID, issued and up to date.'

This time the slap found his other ear, which began to twitch to a disco beat. Mayank leaned on a nearby wall, brain ringing.

'Government ID?' the policeman laughed. 'Even the dog who eats rats outside our station can get government ID. We're finally going to clean the city of you lot.' This was more explanation than the constable had given a prisoner in months. The effort seemed to make him thirsty. He unpocketed a quarter bottle, took a long draught and handed it to his companion. As they drank, Mayank heard them muttering.

'You know the guy I just gave one to?'

'Talks a lot.'

'Yeah. But he's sounding Indian now.'

'What? How would that work?'

'As he's getting sober. First, I couldn't understand a word he was saying. But now he's talking like one of us. He sounds just like my brother-in-law, in fact. That bastard also whines all the time.'

*

'You'll go blind with such cheap booze,' Inspector Chauhan said from behind a long wooden table topped by glass. The ancient computer was on a smaller desk adjacent to Chauhan's and, mystifying to Mayank, faced visitors instead of the policeman. A blue rectangle with white text flickered on the flat screen.

'Yes sir. Made a mistake. Please forgive me.'

'This is what happens if you don't carry your ID. You were passed out. How are we supposed to tell?'

'Yes sir. Made a mistake. Please forgive me.'

A lady police appeared, her leather belt edged with white mould. She dragged a chair to the smaller desk without acknowledging either of them, sat in front of the computer, opened a brown manila folder and began to type with two fingers.

'So, Mayank Tyagi.' A sly smile appeared on Chauhan's face. 'Since you're a Tyagi, what have you sacrificed?'

Mayank thought of a story his grandmother liked to tell, about how the Tyagis had given up their Brahmin status at the behest of the rishi Parashuram. Then he thought of his father. But this, evidently, was the inspector's idea of a rhetorical question. 'Lots of Tyagis in my village, of course,' he went on. 'Where are you from? Where does your family live?'

'Just down the road, sir. Mahipalpur.'

'Mayank from Mahipalpur. I'm also from Mahipalpur,' he said with a smile. 'Too bad you got caught up in all this. What were you doing there, outside the Bengali basti?'

'Sir, we were shooting a YouTube video. I work for a channel. We do reporting on news.'

Chauhan did not bother disguising his disapproval. 'You get drunk and shoot videos? How old are you? Nineteen? Twenty? No college? What does your father do?'

The lady police stood up, her chair scraping loudly against the predawn hush. She walked to a dark corner, towards what Mayank had supposed was a ragged pile of clothes. At the policewoman's approach the bundle began to shiver to life, and he saw now an old woman under there who had wrapped herself against the police station's night-damp in a sari and shawls of indeterminate colour. As the policewoman began some kind of speech the old lady fumbled around until her fingers located a pair of glasses with thick black frames, which she drew slowly to her dark, weathered face.

'My father has expired, sir,' Mayank said. 'After school I went straight to work.'

'When did he expire?' Chauhan asked without any sign of sympathy. It was a response that Mayank infinitely preferred. He felt a kind of respect for this policeman.

'When I was seven.'

'How?'

'Accident, sir. He was walking on the road when a bridge collapsed.'

The inspector started, then leaned back in his chair, studying Mayank's face with a new intensity. 'Mayank Tyagi. You're Sushant's boy?' he said.

'Yes sir. Sushant Tyagi was my father's full name.'

The inspector shook his head, smiling at the enormity of the moment. 'Can't believe it. Good sportsman, your father. When we were young I thought he would join the police like me. Very sad what happened to him. Very sad.'

The conversation between the policewoman and the old lady was acquiring some kind of dramatic weight. There was moaning, head-holding, hands were thrown about. It seemed like the older woman kept trying to get up but was being convinced to stay seated.

Mayank looked at Chauhan, whose expression had turned kindly, or some approximation of kindly. He knew he should feel relief. A few minutes ago, when he was trapped alongside the presumed illegals, Mayank would have delighted in even the loosest connection to any of these uniformed powers, but now that the fear of confinement had passed, now that his nation and nationalism had been established, instead of relief he felt the onset of a familiar burning sensation in his neck and behind his ears. He could sense the next question, and immediately, as if hunting for a way to cordon the thought off, to keep it from spreading like a noxious gas through his mind, he closed his eyes and forced the memory, that childhood moment, his mother behind a desk, behind a chair, standing, forehead and eyes shaded by the widow's ghoonghat, gingerly placing her palms on the back and shoulders of…

'How is your mother keeping?' Chauhan asked. Mayank opened his eyes to see that sly smile playing again at the edges of the policeman's lips. 'It must have been tough for her.' Mayank took a deep breath. Told himself to calm down. He could imagine the conversations once he left this room, once he was allowed to leave. He felt suddenly hollow.

'She is well, thank you. I'll give her your wishes.'

A loud crash came from the corner. The old woman was showing surprising strength, succeeding in fending away the policewoman. She moved swiftly towards where Mayank and the inspector sat, but ultimately the policewoman caught up to her, spinning her around. 'Please,' the old lady entreated, 'he did not mean anything.' She began to repeat this almost as a chant as she was ushered back into her corner, her pleas turning softer and less forceful as she was deposited on to the bench. She pinched the glasses from her nose, muttering all the time, wiping each lens with a fold of her sari, using it again to sop the tears from her face.

Chauhan watched the scene play out with a tranquil expression. He turned to Mayank, shaking his head regretfully.

'Such a sad situation,' he said. 'Maybe it's a good thing you never went to college. Your father would be happy. What all they teach in college nowadays.'

Mayank chose a casual nod, as if he as well felt no regret about that outcome.

'See that poor lady,' Chauhan continued. 'A simple farmer's wife. From Jharkhand. What was her mistake? She put her son in school. He did well. Went to college. Did so well he could come to Delhi. Then everything started to go wrong. The professors began to fill the boy's head with nonsense. Did you see the media outside when they brought you in?'

Mayank remembered the clamour as the police van pulled into the compound, the van rocking until foreign and domestic detainees alike were clutching the sides as if they might prevent it from keeling over. 'Didn't see, but I heard.' He felt the despair in his stomach once again. 'Is that ... do you have that student here? The union leader?'

'Yes. This is why those vultures have gathered.' Chauhan paused as if to ponder, leaning back in his chair, running the tip of his thumbnail along the serrated rim of his forefinger's nail, creating a rasp that seemed to fill the dawn. 'Now this woman is refusing to leave. Says she'll only go with her son. We're letting her rest. We'll kick her out tomorrow.'

Mayank studied the mother. She was silent in the corner. The union leader had black hair and a shiny beard but his mother's face was small in the same way, close-set eyes and thick nose. He thought about what his own mother might do if he was in this situation. He felt a dim sense of culpability but he could not place it as such; it was, to him, like a gnawing sensation around his upper neck, somewhere near the back of his brain.

3

MAYANK WALKED OUT OF THE police building as the sky was edging towards first redness. The compound was empty now save for a few white cars and, in the dust underneath the large lamps, heaps of tiny winged blackflies that had expired overnight. Mayank had seen piles of these corpses before and he associated them with the arrival of Diwali, the thought of which brought a small hit of pleasure. He walked underneath the discordant red-and-blue signage of the archway feeling unshackled, though he'd never been in real danger, he told himself – or was it that he'd managed the danger pretty well?

He was getting too old for firecrackers. Instead of going to his uncle's, climbing to the smoky rooftop where his cousins were playing, spending his evening scampering between eruptions of light and sound and whistling cordite rockets and longing silently for the neighbour's daughter, who each year appeared in a daring new salwar kameez, maybe he'd ask his mother to make a special Diwali dinner this year. They could spend it at home. This seemed important, suddenly.

At the crossing of Vasant Kunj and Nelson Mandela Marg, where last night Sushil and he sat under the flyover and drank, he saw for the first time a green sign advertising a climbing centre and was briefly mystified. He should've turned right for home, he'd barely had any sleep, but instead he took a left, crossing a management school and a South Indian restaurant and then the shuttered shops of Masoodpur market, the unlit signs promising underwear, bathroom tiles, physics foundation courses. This stretch of road, the small shops and eateries of Masoodpur market, reminded him of what his own village, Mahipalpur, had looked like when he was a boy. It was strange to think about. A long time ago, well before he was born, some time in his father's youth most likely, both these urban villages had been bisected by the same road, the four-lane Vasant Kunj road. In both villages the people who owned land along the road had become rich, left the farm life behind, joined the new world, starting their own businesses or selling ancestral parcels. Mahipalpur just happened to fall on the side close to the Gurgaon highway and the sprawling new airport. This meant that his own village had changed far faster in appearance. Changed a few times, in fact. When he was a boy, he would obtain sweets and Pepsi on credit from the storekeepers along the main road. Now there were backpacker cafes, outlet stores, massage parlours, nightclubs like the one Bhavna went to. Maybe his life would've been very different if his family had been from Masoodpur. He felt grateful that modernity had blessed him in this way, blessed them all.

He'd been walking a long time. The orange-toffee sun had lain a tincture of sweat upon his skin. In the distance, at Andheria Mod, he could see the boxy white metro station. A next transformation already underway. Recently he'd read in the news that the government had purchased a special boring machine to create perhaps the country's widest tunnel, a large section of it passing directly underneath his ancestral village. Six lanes of cars would travel many kilometres, diving in at the junction he'd just left and emerging at the giant statue of Lord Shiva along the highway. It would really help with the traffic, Mayank thought, which turned malevolent every morning and evening, even on weekends. Maybe some of the shops and businesses that had come up to serve the big-car folk would now close, maybe some businesses that better served their own community would once again open. It was coming on to a quarter-past five. As he hurried up the steps leading to the metro station

Mayank remembered a line from that news article which had made him strangely proud. For a long time now, maybe as long as he'd been alive, Mayank had assumed that people were powerless in the face of change. Much of the change wrought in his little urban village had been occasioned by a developmental decision, taken in an unknown office at an unknown time, building a road that connected the city proper to the new highway. There had been just one sentence in that news article that spoke of so much else, but it made him feel stronger, a reminder of the resolute stock he came from. He remembered the line verbatim: *Widening of the existing road passing through the village is almost impossible due to heavy settlement.* So they had fought, his people, the first settlers of this land, against the final impingement, an evisceration, and the government had relented, forced underground to achieve its spectral ends.

The train to Central Secretariat arrived a minute before schedule. Mayank stepped into the sleek off-white interior and took a seat near a large window tinted blue, facing an identical window so he could watch the shabby buildings of the outer city transform into gleaming mirrored structures as they rode. Far along the corridor-like compartment an early bird dozed, head lolling against an advertisement, but other than that Mayank seemed to be alone. The phone in his trouser pocket buzzed with an alert. This he ignored. An hour or so ago, when Chauhan had handed back his phone, Mayank noted that Sushil had tried him multiple times over the course of the night. Sushil had also sent a number of messages, which remained unread. Mayank felt no rancour. But he felt no desire to speak to his friend at this moment. The sudden vibration against his thigh had reminded him as well that there was the matter of messaging Kashyap. Mayank knew he was not making it to work today. He was too tired. Not physically exhausted, he felt instead giddy and energized. This was an anticipatory exhaustion, occasioned by the conversations that would ensue, explanations, jokes, perhaps even a bout of sympathy, all which he wanted none of.

It took the train about thirty minutes to pull up under the great bisected dome of Central Secretariat station. Mayank hopped over the yellow stripe that ran along the edge as people bundled inside. A shaft of white light warmed the platform stone. As he made his way to the violet line, which everyone, including the station announcers, rhymed with toilet, Mayank, who had looked up the pronunciation in a fit of sadness at thirteen, was instead put in mind of the word violent. It was so strange, this language, like this train, where it started, where it ended up.

He stood upon a purple arrow until the train arrived. There were many more passengers, but Mayank found a seat easily. His eye fell again and again on lurid purple markings, little dashes and circles, the hammering and digging and bridging long complete so that this violet vessel had become vital to the body of this city, carrying thousands every day. As the stations ticked away a growing sensation of worry began to manifest as an intense fidgetiness, perhaps in mind more than body, and he fought the desire to take out his phone, his customary panacea. It felt important, this morning, vitally important to stay in the moment, to fight the urge to retreat into a screen like some kid playing Jetpack Joyride. The train deposited a load of passengers at Lajpat Nagar and suffered a small influx hunting for seats. As they approached Moolchand the dread he had been feeling magnified into a genuine sweat, fatigue and hunger and disgust from the night before turning into a dizziness that threatened to take him out, if he'd been standing his knees would surely have buckled, and a snatch of overheard conversation came back to him from far into his childhood, so long ago that the memory might've been manufactured, Papa addressing Chhote Chacha: 'My son's going to be prime minister one day.' Mayank had been to the exact site at ground level but here in the smooth effacing train he could never quite tell where the girder had collapsed, where the hard heft of a bridge had found his father as he attempted to cross the road. Mayank felt angry. What a silly thing for his father to say just because he'd brought home a topping score. Perhaps a boy like him could one day be prime minister but Mayank had no idea, no conception how to get there, how to fulfil his father's ambition. It seemed sometimes to him that this long engagement with Kashyap was to be found somewhere in the tapestry that had started threading out from that moment, as if the tiny trumpet and his grandstanding show could bring Mayank closer somehow to the centre of power, the centre of safety.

In the years that followed it had been difficult to figure out who to blame. Soon after his eleventh birthday Mayank began to consume anything he could find online about the accident. There were a few grainy news clips. As the anchor briefed the viewers enormous yellow cranes incised into the rubble. No more bodies were recovered after the first haul. The South Indian bureaucrat the media called Metro Man would appear at the end of some of the clips, giving a press conference, and with distance it came to seem to Mayank a genuine expression of grief; the man had even tried to resign, which was unheard of, but the politicians didn't let him, they made him continue until the project was complete. Years later he read that the Metro Man had in fact tried to retire in 2005, well before this carnage. Perhaps things would've been different if they'd let him. The construction company had an American name but was based out of Hong Kong. Their representative stated that a manager had been terminated and argued that such incidents were bound to happen when working in such an extraordinary rush, with the government insisting that this phase had to be complete before the upcoming Commonwealth Games.

The recorded announcement indicated that the next station was Jasola Apollo. The train was well past the accident site now. Mayank knew he should get off, he had no reason or desire to travel to this end of the city, to see, through the facing window, not gleaming cars and malls but crumbling apartment complexes and the pallor of desert dust. In the months that followed the accident, as the Delhi government was working out the final compensation package, Mayank's mother received a notification from the Ministry that they would have to evacuate the flat. Panic. She contacted another widow, a woman who had helped them that August and September with the terrifying paperwork and proofs they needed to claim the pension. This woman, whom Mayank remembered as fair, large-eyed, fleshy and cheerful, informed them that it was not a bureaucrat from his father's department but instead someone at the Ministry of Housing and Urban Poverty Alleviation who would decide. She gave his mother a name and then whispered something in her ear. 'Take your boy,' she called out, as she was leaving the room. 'I took both my children.'

Again Mayank thought to get off the train, but he could feel the futility of that act, with nowhere to go, no one to meet. He had begun to suspect that he had no real friends, no one he could stand with when things got tough. At Old Faridabad station a family of four got on board, taking the bench opposite him. Oiled hair gleaming under the train lights, the girls in matching salwars and pigtails. The father had hauled in a large metal trunk, which he guarded by placing a palm on it. Mayank looked up at the violet line plastered to the wall of the compartment and noted that the station was connected to the national rail network. He thought about talking to the father. Surely they wanted the train going the other way, into the city, to see the centre of the great capital, its shaded pathways and monuments to authority.

Mayank had gone with his mother, as instructed, to the office of the functionary at the Ministry of Housing. It was a small room, no air conditioning, a wooden clock shaped like India on the wall, the only furniture a big desk and four plastic chairs. As Mayank played Jetpack

Joyride on his mother's phone, racking up one of his highest scores, the bureaucrat smiled and spoke to his mother in a sympathetic tone but explained that there was nothing he could do. At one point, as Mayank flew after a golden pig shedding glittering golden coins, his mother walked around the large desk so now she stood behind the man they'd come to see. Mayank sensed rather than saw this movement, his own focus was taken by this pig, this chase, so he only heard little grunts of satisfaction and, once, a moan of pained pleasure. They left the office soon after, and on the way home his mother snarled something about this being the only way, the other widows had also succumbed, didn't he see, that's why she'd needed him there, that's why they took their children, why was he silent, why didn't he understand? The matter would have ended there, should have, except the bureaucrat had recently purchased a new phone, one with a lens, one of those crappy early cameras that produced blocky pixelated footage. Mayank felt grateful, now, that this was in the time before social media. The short video of his mother massaging the bureaucrat's shoulders and neck made it to the world as an MMS. Someone had titled it 'Massage in Ministry'. It was a lucky thing the bureaucrat had positioned the camera on a shelf towards the far wall so you could not really see his mother's face, lucky also that her face was covered, that she still wore the ghoonghat of the bereaved. Framed front and centre, the bureaucrat was easily identifiable and sacked within weeks. Funny, perhaps, the way the older boys of his neighbourhood made the connection: you could see, quiet in one corner, nine-year-old Mayank bent over a screen playing Jetpack Joyride.

For the most part now Mayank fights successfully against his mind's desire to return to that time. It is imaginary, this damage, our past and future are both imagined, we fabricate the very fabric of our lives. Only when he is exhausted does it come over him. His lasting regret is that it all unfolded so quickly, that in his failure to protect his mother he did not have time to grieve the father.

4

'NOW THE BASTARD REMEMBERS HIS country?' Kashyap growled. 'For so many years not one post. Ever since he had that tax issue last year, he's been waving the flag.'

Things were tense. A video released by Mayank's favourite YouTuber, a bodybuilding influencer named Captain Flight, had achieved new measures of virality. More than forty-eight hours after it was posted the algorithm still pushed the video Mayank's way. The way of everyone they knew, it seemed. There were reaction videos by plenty of other influencers marvelling at the audacious original – 'Suck ups, all of them,' Kashyap explained – while a half-dozen episodic vlogs that detailed the preparations, each with their own mini-arcs, were already at a million plus views per post. A patriotic hashtag contrived by the former pilot had embedded, doing the rounds on Twitter and Facebook. Captain Flight already had a commanding following, somewhere between six and seven million, but this set of videos had moved beyond his own followers, showing up on the feeds of people who'd never heard of him.

'It seems to be getting views in America, Europe,' Mayank said.

'Comments from the UK,' Sushil added helpfully.

'That's what we need to target!' Kashyap shouted. 'So many of us abroad, but we still don't get views outside the country. You know how much money an American view gets? Ten times an Indian. Captain has cashed in.'

'It must have cost him, though. Going to America. Renting a plane,' said Sushil.

'True,' Kashyap said. This seemed to cheer him up. 'And it's not like I know how to fly. I could've done it in a car, I suppose. Or on a bike.'

Mayank looked up at his boss. 'How did he get the flight plan approved? Imagine trying it in India.'

It was true that it seemed faintly peculiar. Yet Mayank consumed video after video, watching Captain Flight and his wife negotiate American airports, AI bag scanners, extortionate doughnut prices, long-distance Ubers. One of the attractions to the audience, he realized, was that the videos offered an authentic glimpse into the American heartland. The captain had gone abroad with specific purpose: to fly a three-hour route that would inscribe an assiduous map of India among the clouds over Florida, at least a fair bit of Florida. Aviation nerds around the world had taken note, tracking the journey on flight scanners. The disjunct that Mayank had hazily identified had to do with this act of inscription: planting one map on to another, one body upon another. Later Mayank looked up some of the names that the plane had journeyed over, claimed, in a sense, rural reaches named after old forts, long stretches of highway, a ghost town once famous for phosphate mining but now emptied of its people. One place that called itself a city but that Wikipedia said had 814 families. America truly was a strange place.

'In the post, he couldn't show the full map,' Mayank pointed out. 'Of America, I mean. They only posted a zoomed-in version. Against the full map of America, that route of India that Captain Flight flew would look so tiny. It wouldn't have the same effect.'

'That's true!' Kashyap exclaimed. He began a quiet cogitation. 'We should hit him with a response vid. Should we hit him with a response? Will it seem like a cheap shot? He's put in all that effort and money while we're sitting here holding our dicks.' He closed his eyes and took a slow, deep breath. Then he turned to the pair. 'An important lesson for you to remember, boys. Wait for the right moment. This is his moment. People are appreciating. Media is covering it. One day we'll get him. One day I'll get all the pretenders. Fuck YouTube anyway, fucking cheapskates, they'll be dead soon, the way they're going.'

Mayank had noticed this tendency, the way Kashyap's mind could rearrange the realities of the outside world to align perfectly with what he was thinking. Today he was down on YouTube, so YouTube was dying. When one of their videos next went viral the site would once again become a godly force, vanquisher of old media and elite control.

It was even a little embarrassing, Mayank felt, that Kashyap was so competitive. The follower counts were so far apart that Flight could very reasonably never have seen Kashyap's show or even heard of his existence. Kashyap had been inspired by the American shock masters, Limbaugh, Carlsen, Bongino, he could put out a video every day if he wanted; Captain Flight preferred elaborate set-ups, big entertainment, a scale of ambition that spoke directly to his country's prevailing repressions. Mayank could see what Kashyap craved. The big blast. The jump into top gear. All his life Mayank had craved the same thing. Now he felt unsure.

He was working out details for the show's next video, forty minutes on the extrajudicial killings in Uttar Pradesh, much of the airtime focused on making fun of all those who were getting themselves into a sweat as if they couldn't see just how that lawless jungle was turning around, when Sushil walked up to his desk. His colleague had a curious expression on his face.

'Bro, you seen this?' he said, handing Mayank his phone.

Mayank studied the Instagram post with a sinking heart. The creator of the poll was related to Nisha Bisht – her sister, in fact. One of those side-by-side comparisons. This lady put a pointed question to her followers: *Does this channel's Bharat Mata look like my sister? Yes. No. Don't Waste My Time.*

Sixty-five per cent of the respondents agreed. There were an outrageous number of votes. Mayank felt his stomach perform a slow flip. An imagined cacophony seemed to grow in his ears. Some comments pointed to different features of the face that did not match up. There was a protracted discussion about the shape of the nose that was threatening to turn unseemly. Why did all these people care? Couldn't the internet for once shut up. It was a little thing, a pebble kicked over the loose-earthed side of a slope. How could it have resulted in this? He was not responsible for the work of nature or for the nature of man. A complicated emotion began to well up within, one side pushing forward and free, he had not done anything wrong, the other still, strapped in place, paretic with car-crash guilt.

'Vikram sir will lose it if he sees,' Sushil whispered. 'What should we do?'

Rupa had also linked to a video, a reaction post she'd made to the events of the past few days. Mayank felt speechless, stupefied. He clicked.

5

SASU HAD BEEN KILLED. RUN over by a car, she said. Billoo masi phoned Mayank herself, though he wasn't sure if this was to gloat or inform or make sure action was taken. When she caught him at night outside their building with the pups, Billoo masi always said to him, 'You feed. Your responsibility.' At least she didn't call the cops on Mayank for feeding strays, as one neighbour had. When the police had showed up Mayank used the Prime Minister's first lockdown speech as his defence. No way the cop was arguing. But now as he tied his sneakers, trying to figure out what to do, he felt a strong sense of futility. It was coming on to four in the afternoon. As he stepped outside the apartment the comforting background clatter of firecrackers rose in volume into something strident and visceral, a thick smoke he barely noticed flying swiftly to the back of his throat.

No one would come on Diwali. He'd have to pick Sasu off the side of the road himself. What to do with him then? Ultimately, he decided on a park that was a fair walk away, quite like the one he'd lain in a few nights ago. Someone had dragged the body to the side of the road. Mayank could see, from the distended midriff, that he'd been hit in the haunches by the Innova, shattering his rib cage. Cars went by. Suddenly it seemed very important to get Sasu out of that spot. He folded the little corpse into a towel he'd taken from the linen drawer. A pair of large dumpsters sat in an open-air enclosure along one wall of this park. It would've been nice to take Sasu to a water body, to allow him to float in dignity into the horizon like some ancient deity or medieval warrior, but there was nothing suitable around, nothing he could get to fast enough. As he pushed through the last-minute shopping rush it seemed like everyone knew what he was carrying in his folded arms, rearing back grimly until he was past. When Mayank got to the dumpsters, he saw blood had seeped through, staining his T-shirt fuchsia.

He walked back home slowly, allowing the rounds of celebratory explosion to return him to a better mood – how cool his neighbourhood seemed today, smoke clinging low to the ground, battered buildings, a sharp alluring aroma of cordite everywhere and the whistle, spurt and ratatat of firecrackers slowly solidifying the impression that he was no longer at home but somewhere more thrilling, walking a dangerous map in *Call of Duty* perhaps.

Had he doomed the boy, naming him Sasuke? Was it inevitable that Sasu would be the one dashing out on to that devilish main road? Does the name lead our way, or do we grow into the name? When it was clear that the pups would not be homed, Mayank had decided to give them names. His favourite he'd named Naru after Naruto, the eponymous protagonist of the manga series that he'd watched every day after school as a kid. As a pup Naru had a blonde fringe, short spikes of yellow-brown hair just above his eyes. He was brave and rather stupid, which also seemed right. Mayank felt a shot of gratitude that the car didn't get Naru, then immediately felt guilty. For a moment he fell back to his childhood, recalling the excitement with which they would discuss the previous day's episode each day in school, leaping and hurling about the classroom during break, and then he remembered a feeling that had struck deeper still, a sharp current of pride and something akin to joy when, while watching, he came upon a moment when the religious system of Naruto's clan seemed to match his own, the chakras, for example, they used, which had clearly been borrowed from the Vedic rishis, the Deva path and the Asura, even Sasuke's summon, the huge hawk Garuda.

Sasu was the one who always charged at his mother as soon as she appeared. Sprinting on his tiny legs he would hurl himself upon her at full pelt as if he could scarcely register that she was back, nipping at her neck and shoulders until she growled a warning, yielding the nipples on her belly in disgust. Mayank was not sure why the mother stopped appearing, if her milk had dried up or she'd become sick of being torn apart by the little razor teeth of her children. It seemed to make sense, especially after he'd arrived at the first name, to call this one Sasu, after Sasuke, a handsome, deeply talented ninja, but troubled, errant, unable to respect authority. The girl pup's name came easy then, Sakura, and the runt he'd name Boru, Boruto from the later series, Naruto's heroic son.

It was almost dark. The shops were crammed with crowd, halogen signboards blazing, every structure strung with red or yellow bulbs and the air with a roasted taste. In a few homes traditional diyas flickered upon their parapets, fighting the wind, and as ever on the night before Diwali the moon was amber yellow and at the delicate last of its wane. Mayank noticed the slender crescent emerge from grey cloud and smiled to himself.

Most of his life he'd felt an affection for the moon — that was what his name meant, after all. Mayank's father had chosen the name. He would bring the word to its Sanskrit roots: the shining moon. Through his childhood Mayank obsessed lightly about the distant lunar being. He would watch it grow and recede and feel a corresponding fullness in his chest. He noted that it shifted in colour, from white to dull yellow, sometimes even to orange, and that this seemed arbitrary compared to its rigid regime of shape. In later years he looked at the scars of teenage acne upon its visage and found them as inevitable as his own. In class one morning Mr Pandey the science teacher had informed them that the moon had no light of its own, that the light we observed was simply a reflection of sunlight. Mayank refused to believe this. He stood up and argued that this could not be the case. The teacher was adamant, and Mayank got irate and incoherent and would not stop until finally he ran from class on the verge of tears. He could remember also the undernote, an inexplicable residue, the sure sense that Pandey was telling the class that it was not the moon but Mayank who was deficient, and the man who'd given his boy this name a reflection rather than light.

What will you do? The message arrived on his phone as Mayank was turning on to his street. He could see the sneer with which Kashyap had surely typed those words.

The follow-up arrived rapidly. *I gave you a chance when no one would.*

Things had become tense around the office yesterday morning, when they'd discovered the poll. Nothing doing, Kashyap said, refusing to consider any form of apology. Perhaps he remembered the conversation between the two of them the day that Mayank first came across Nisha's feed, the assenting nod he'd given. Culpability, implications, both legal and monetary, such were the considerations of a person with something to lose, of a person who has achieved some status in life, Kashyap implied with a smarmy smile, outside the ken of a young fellow like you, and when Mayank had persisted that smile turned into something nasty and threatening, no longer was it a smile, it became a goading sneer that was swiftly followed by a challenge to both masculinity and intelligence: what kind of limpdick cares about a girl who doesn't even know his name?

It had occurred to Mayank in lock-up that he needed to stop trying to prove himself to this man or he would wind up in worse places than the Bengali basti. Over the course of the night Mayank had felt the fight leach out of him. But he did not like that his own conduct had to be proscribed. Why couldn't he write to Nisha and say sorry if he wanted? It was his error, his hurry. The diktat issued by Kashyap seemed a direct challenge to his sense of himself. He had to remember who he was. Had to remember the experiences that had shaped him, that had for better or worse made him. Somewhere deep inside he knew that his need to apologize drew from the tumult and shame that had once engulfed him and his mother. He sensed as well that this shame he carried inside did not lie that deep. It sat right beneath the surface of his skin, waiting like blood for the smallest opening to ooze out into the world, to show itself. Maybe this shame was in fact his most noticeable feature, the thing that people who knew him saw when they looked into his face, maybe this wound had defined him, had become the very thing that people thought of when they thought of him.

Sushil had tried to help, Mayank had to give him that. After the argument Kashyap returned to his cabin. Mayank sat seething at his desk. The violence of their thoughts seemed to frizz through the air. Sushil stood up with a noisy scrape. He gently closed his eyes, nodded, tapped his chest at his heart three times as if to say, let me handle this, and went quietly into the cabin. The low walls of the cabin meant that Mayank heard the conversation in its entirety. It was this very thing that Sushil said to Kashyap – it must be because of his mother, right, because of what happened to her. To his family. Kashyap claimed he'd forgotten about it completely. The sound of pursed lips smacking in commiseration. That was probably Sushil, Mayank thought later, because Kashyap would not budge even at this.

Mayank unlocked his phone and found the icon for WhatsApp. *I should never have followed someone as selfish and single-minded as you,* he typed. He erased these words and put the phone back into his pocket. Kashyap could wait. He didn't like waiting. Walking the steps up to his apartment, Mayank was nagged by another memory. As he sifted through the sands of the manic past weeks he came to a round hard pebble. Thick black frames, silver squares that occluded her eyes. Lines on her dark face, flesh folding around the jaw despite the gaunt cheeks. Mayank realized he didn't give a shit about the student union leader, not really. He couldn't care if that man was kept in prison or released, if he was guilty or innocent. It was the old lady he remembered now. Unwavering in her love. Unwilling to leave. That was his doing too, in a way. The limitless consequences of little actions.

He washed his face, shaved, then bathed for a long time, using three buckets, relishing the warmth of the water. This was usually a sign that winter would arrive soon. He felt very clean. Diwali was a good time for a new start, he told himself. He could not think what was next, which made him fearful, but he knew it was important to focus on the positives. This home, family, his favourite festival. He dressed carefully in a kurta pajama the shade of wine, applied some cologne, and went to the living room to see his mother.

Sharp yellow light. Gleaming tap above the gleaming sink. A vase with plastic flowers upon the fridge. Turmeric and sandalwood floating from her favourite incense. The patterned plastic sheet that covered the dining table was askew, one end further to the ground by two or three inches, an anomaly his mother appeared unable to rectify. She took him to the small wooden temple mounted on the wall, where the blue smoke curling to the ceiling left faint grey streaks like fingermarks. They performed their obeisance. When she reached up to thumb the tilak on to his forehead she noticed him muttering.

'What is it?' she asked, as they sat at the dining table.

'I think I'm going to quit,' Mayank said. 'That man is driving me crazy.'

She took his right hand in hers, inspecting his knuckles and fingers. 'Something or the other you'll find. People like that only know how to bully.'

You'll be nothing without me.

Go back to making videos no one will ever watch.

The man was relentless. Even without inducement, even on Diwali, Kashyap seemed to have a fund of anger he could tap into. The firecrackers reached their evening crescendo, a resounding, reassuring racket that arrived from every direction. The windows were closed but the air was scorched grey even inside the apartment. For some minutes talk was pointless.

'Do you remember what I told you,' Mayank said in the next lull, 'about that girl whose photo we used for the Bharat Mata vid?'

'Yes,' his mother said. 'You showed me the photo. Nice girl.'

'You don't understand,' Mayank said miserably. 'She hates me. She would hate me if she knew.'

'How did she find out?'

It occurred to Mayank for the first time that his mother's experiences might have given her an acute sense of the nature of technology, the possibilities and judgements it offered.

'There's no harm in getting in touch. Tell her how you feel,' his mother said. A long line of detonations from a firecracker comprising red cartridges stuffed with saltpetre secured to a central thread, ladders that seemed to grow longer every year, two thousand, five thousand, ten thousand, prices jumping steeply so that the maximum available length was a more reliable indicator of general prosperity, Mayank had once heard a stand-up on TV say, than the Nifty and Sensex. 'You don't have to post it on social media,' she shouted. 'Just send her a message. Be honest.'

*

Mayank was so full he wanted to lie on the couch with his phone out and pajama knot loosened, but the pups would be scared. They'd just lost their brother. This incessant shelling. Sasu might well have been chased out of some hole by a chocolate bomb, a spinning wheel, even the whooshed eruption of a fountain of fire. Mayank ladled rice into three bowls, added gravy, leftover beans, meticulously shared out the massive pile of bones he'd purchased a few days ago off Qureshi and left to soak in a watery dal soup.

They refused to come out from their hiding place under the stairs. How cute though, with their little faces burrowed into the pair of old blankets his mother had deemed fit for the purpose. He squatted there for some minutes, wheedling, gently prodding, until a whimpering Naru emerged. A bomb exploded and he charged back into the darkness, but then he came out much quicker, bringing his siblings with him. Mayank let them at the bowls, laughing at their greed. Last year on Diwali a famous actress had complained about how the firecrackers in Mumbai scared her dog. Great anger.

Mayank had helped Kashyap plan the channel's response. How dare she criticize the greatest of all festivals, the return of the king? Did she say this about Christmas – didn't turkeys have rights? When the Peacefuls chopped the heads off thousands of goats every year? Mayank sourced images of her in leather. He found one tantalizing clip of her gyrating in a leopard print Tarzan skirt and bikini top. Strictly speaking there was no cruelty to animals in that last clip, but it gave the video the perfect thumbnail.

He plonked himself in the dust, granting all three nibbles of his fingers and wrists, when a familiar voice came in above him. 'Happy Diwali, Mayank,' said Bhavna. She glimmered against the dark. A modest peacock-blue salwar kameez had been matched with a thick rim of turquoise eyeshadow and sparkling danglers. Even her feet looked pretty, toe rings, low heels, bright polish. Mayank jumped up. He brushed the dust off his backside. 'Nice kurta,' she said, smiling, and this time it didn't seem like she was mocking him.

'Thank you,' he said. 'Happy Diwali to you.' He was trying to think of the right compliment when he noticed Bhavna's parents were standing a few feet behind her. 'Happy Diwali, uncle, aunty,' he said, smiling.

Bhavna's father gave him a sour look and walked on. The mother smiled at him, nodding, lifted the hem of her sari to avoid catching the dust. 'Happy Diwali, beta,' she said, once she'd negotiated a tricky rut in the road. Bhavna began to follow, raising a quizzical eyebrow.

Mayank stared at the retreating blue figure. 'I'm getting a new job,' he called out. 'If I get it, let's celebrate.'

Bhavna turned, smiling. 'All the time working. Sure. Let's celebrate.'

He felt grateful she had not brought up ScooterSerf. At home he peeled off his kurta pajama, which smelled sharply of smoke though he hadn't played, not even a sparkler. Brushed, took a bath, changed into nightclothes, settled into bed and opened his laptop. The company he wanted to apply to was a new venture opened up by an offshoot of Google. They had just acquired a warehouse space at the border of Mahipalpur, where village met highway. It was a computer vision firm, helping to refine vision language models. A warehouse floor that once held cartons of cigarettes, shampoos, shower gels and biscuits would now house a hundred or more desks where young workers would put identifying tags on image after image. Through these tags, artificial intelligences could read what an image contained. Mayank thought of the cheap AI app that had sent an arrow flying into the heart of Nisha's life. If Mayank got the job he would be naming different kinds of trees, mountains, cats, cars, helping these machines learn the difference between a rivulet and the outflow of a standpipe. The job listing promised real money, dollar money, like the call centres of twenty years ago.

So this is how those fearsome intelligences are being built, Mayank thought. Mayank remembered the Mughals, the celebrated palaces and mausoleums the invader emperors had constructed using the hardened hands of poor Hindus. Perhaps every kind of great monument had to be erected this way. These companies were the new invaders, bearing sunny Californian names and dollar deposits, yet once again it was the rough work of people like him that would create the scaffolding upon which towering transformations would occur. You had to do the work well, with attention and pride. Nisha deserved at least that.

FOUR

1

A NERVY MORNING. NISHA CAME in early to make sure the cleaning crew had not missed the marble countertops. She inspected the shop glass for smudges, adjusted the alignment of a few display boxes that had mysteriously shifted over the course of the night. By the double door a long piece of thread had snagged in the carpet, perhaps from a chunni, a spit of scarlet river in a salt pan desert. Once everything was satisfactory Nisha had the delicate task of sending Deven to the chemist on the ground floor to procure a can of Axe. Siddharth had discussed the odour issue with Deven before. Nisha had some sympathy. Deven had an incredibly long commute, a couple of buses before the metro, coming in from Mangolpuri, beyond Paschim Vihar. He was deeply dark, maybe the darkest man she'd seen, with hairy hands and neck. It seemed natural to her that he would sweat a lot, which enhanced her sense of pity. When she said it, he took a step back, jamming one leg tight against the other. Then he walked away briskly. It would've been easier coming from a man, Nisha knew, at least coming from the manager, but Siddharth was already in some corporate tower, probably in a new suit, trying to pretend he belonged.

Mrs Jain arrived just after 11.30, in keeping with the detailed schedule that had been shared over email. A new assistant in tow. The shop's solitary customer was almost at the counter so Nisha smiled at the big boss but kept her focus on him, a tall youngish man with a stooped back. Mrs Jain nodded, pleased, which made Nisha blush. Mrs Jain was slim, glamorous, a South Bombay institution who today had favoured a floral jumpsuit that revealed muscular shoulders. Her bag was a Chanel flap that Nisha had seen on Instagram, not more than a day or two ago, in Alia Bhatt's hand.

'I had a bunch of meetings today,' Mrs Jain said, 'but I thought I should visit. The new manager won't come in for another…' She looked at her assistant, a short, bespectacled woman with a fountain of grey hair that might've been the brainchild of a hairdresser.

'Two weeks,' the assistant said.

'I hope everything has been running smoothly?' Mrs Jain continued.

'Yes ma'am, all fine. Anyway Siddharth sir was around for the Diwali rush,' Nisha said. 'It's only been a few days.'

But in truth it had been tough without Siddharth. Especially with all that nonsense online, so many random people talking about her like they were discussing a character on a TV show. Nisha tried hard to block it out but it seemed, when she checked, like she was submerged, floundering for footing as the waves crashed into her, comments, speculation, comparisons, casually thrown invective. It was a terrifying sensation, and she was grateful to have her work, which came to feel like a sanctuary; she appreciated for the first time the simple discipline her job asked, wake up, show up, give your utmost. Nothing mattered but the customer. Here she felt in control. She could prepare.

The absence felt vast. Nisha had not realized how much of her workday had been taken up with thoughts of Siddharth. She missed observing how he gently drew a customer in. She missed his workplace demeanour, a permanent smile that she'd learned to read, so that she felt she knew when he was getting anxious, or annoyed with a prevaricator. He was cool in a crisis. Like that time three bearded men had shown up, pushing Deven's predecessor around, demanding they dismantle the

Valentine's Day display. There were smaller things she remembered. When they were standing in position with no one in the shop Siddharth would sometimes drift away, absently using a fingernail to pick at dried matter that had collected on the rim of his nostrils, flicking the scrapings away without even checking if anyone was looking. She had tried to explain once, in bed, how a moment like that brought them closer, but he turned away, aggrieved, it seemed. The rest of that week she had laughed loudly at Siddharth's jokes, made encouraging sounds during meetings, blushingly looked away when he caught her staring, trying to restore to him, she saw now, the sense that he was flawless in her eyes.

That memory left a bitter taste. But she felt especially foolish about how worried she'd been in the week preceding the sunderance, fighting with herself over whether to tell him or not. What a fool she'd been and how lucky that it turned out the way it did, that there was never any need to bring it up with Siddharth. He would've been furious, convinced she was trying to lure him back in, to keep him from going to Mumbai. Nisha took a sharp breath. What if her body had played a trick on her? Perhaps it had sensed before she did that Siddharth was going, had tried to find some way to keep things alive. For a moment that felt true, and she felt ashamed. She chided herself for the foolish, uneducated thought.

The assistant was beckoning her. Nisha walked to the standalone counter Mrs Jain stood next to, the Chanel tossed on to the tabletop as she texted. Mrs Jain laughed, eyes sparkling, and from her phone came a little beep that suggested an emoji had been dropped. She looked up at Nisha, and the smile slowly left her face.

'There are two weeks before the new manager comes in. Until then you're in charge.' She drew her assistant into the conversation. 'And this is our flagship, you know. Here in Delhi. So she has double the responsibility.'

'Yes ma'am. Siddharth sir told me before he left.'

'I know it's only been a few days, but I hope you've had a chance to take a look at the numbers?'

'Numbers?'

'Targets versus actuals,' Mrs Jain said with a note of exasperation. She shook her head. 'Siddharth didn't explain?'

'Yes ma'am, he did. Actually, I used to help him with it before also. Trying to make sure we didn't order too much, too little.' Mrs Jain was studying her closely now. Nisha felt the tops of her cheeks get hot. She took a deep, silent breath. 'Last year, just after Diwali, our sales fell quite a lot. Of course, holiday season is over. But last year everyone was still worried about Covid also. We've asked for fewer cartons of the big sellers, but when we were sending the requisition for this month I suggested to Siddharth, let's keep the hampers high. Hampers, gift boxes, we shouldn't reduce too much, even though Diwali is over. Wedding sales. In the papers they were saying that Delhi will see a record number of weddings this winter, the most ever. All the weddings that were delayed last year because of the outbreak are going to happen this winter.'

'Interesting,' Mrs Jain said. Nisha could not decipher the expression on her face.

'Anyway, there's the winter demand,' Nisha said. 'I noticed last year that people buy more chocolate when it's cold. I couldn't understand why, exactly. Maybe because they're not eating ice cream?'

'What a sharp young woman you are,' Mrs Jain exclaimed. A wave of relief so intense that for the briefest of moments Nisha swayed from her knees. 'Strategic thinker. I don't like that defeatist attitude. Weddings are coming. Christmas is coming. Very good, Nisha Bisht. Very good. How long have you been with us?'

'Just over one year, ma'am. Fifteen months, almost.'

'That's quite a long time.' A quizzical expression appeared. 'I can't understand why he would…'

Nisha waited for Mrs Jain to resume. When she did not, the assistant spoke up. 'Who, ma'am? Why would who...?'

'Siddharth. Who used to be the manager here. Such a nice boy he is. I asked him if we should promote internally, since he would be working closely with the new manager. But he suggested no. Find someone from outside. He was just being careful, I guess.' She smiled at Nisha. 'It's a lot of responsibility to put on such young shoulders. Did you like working with him?'

'Yes,' said Nisha. 'Siddharth sir was very good at his job.'

Mrs Jain glanced at her phone, then slid it into her purse, snapping it shut. She turned for the door, glancing briefly at Deven, who was mute and still in a corner, doing his best to avoid their gaze. 'It was nice meeting you both. Take good care of everything,' she called out. She pointed to her assistant. 'If there's an emergency, next two weeks, call Anushka. She'll bring it directly to me. Anushka, leave them your card please.' The assistant nodded, the grey tresses around her face bobbing eagerly. As they were walking out, she spoke to Nisha for the first time. 'You seem like a good worker, so will you allow me to give you some advice?'

Nisha was so taken aback by the compliment that she blushed once again. 'Of course ma'am. Please say.'

The assistant took off her glasses, looked down at the carpet, then put them on again. 'A pretty girl like you, I know you must be on social media all the time,' she said. 'But you can't let that distract you, not at work. This is real life. Your job. Your manager mentioned some social media thing has been on your mind. What is it, some boy? Anyway, that's your business. We don't pry. But all that stuff that happens online, you can't let it affect what happens in your real life. Don't let it distract you. You have a chance here to really go places.'

Nisha was struck silent. Confused and hot. She produced a smile, nodding eagerly as if soaking in the wisdom. 'Thank you ma'am,' she said. 'I'll keep that in mind.' She felt on the verge of tears.

For a good part of the rest of that day Nisha was furious. She was determined to call up Siddharth and tell him exactly what she thought. Nisha had been proud of the fact that she hadn't let the ruckus online affect her work. She had blocked it away, it had nothing to do with her. She had thrown herself into work. Siddharth had a nerve. Even when her breasts had begun to feel swollen, when she'd somehow been certain something was growing inside of her, no one could have guessed, customer nor colleague. In the late afternoon she sent him a text reading, *What a shitty thing to do*. He responded a few minutes later, but she did not check it. She did not check her messages at all until she was on her way home. She felt relieved of a weight, as if Siddharth's absence had felt to her like a physical burden. What was the point, with someone who could do this? That night Nisha realized she was now not even angry. Instead there was a lightness.

2

NISHA LAY IN BED, TRYING to recover the past few days, which seemed to have slipped from her grasp – or was it life that was skidding somewhere out of control? Shobita was out with her boyfriend. Nisha was glad for the chance to be alone. She closed her eyes, drawing the bedcover tighter over herself, one part of her mind tuned to the cyclic hum of the fan; she thought back to the previous morning, when they'd congregated on the group call. Rupa had called her, then summoned Manoj, who appeared after a brief interim, sunglasses on his forehead, his narrow face blocky in front of a blank blue-grey wall. Before she added Manoj, Rupa had mentioned in passing the squabble he'd been having with his editor, who would only pay half the hotel rate though it was one of Ranikhet's cheapest rooms, and now Nisha could not fail to notice the grime edging the pillowcase behind her brother-in-law's back.

But first she'd tried an upbeat tone. 'How's it going, bhinju? Getting your story?'

'Did you tell her?' Manoj asked his wife.

'Yes, she knows,' Rupa said.

'I couldn't understand it, when I first saw,' Manoj said. 'How she could have your face. That image was all over your cousin's WhatsApp group. Then I saw on Facebook. People were reposting the GIF and getting angrier and angrier. But it looked so much like you. I had to send it to Rupa.'

'It's so strange. Crazy coincidence,' Rupa said. 'She even has your birthmark on her cheek. In the exact same spot. Bizarre.'

The mole was undeniable. How on earth had it appeared in the same location as her own, especially when this AI image had so much else of her already. Not quite everything. A new and improved her. The eyes were a touch rounder and untired, stroking gently upwards, bow lips perfect, yet even the nose, which the computer-mind had noticeably sharpened, seemed of a piece with the nose she'd studied so often in the mirror. There was no wear, that was the other thing, she looked as fresh as sixteen. This felt like an infringement in itself. She had not requested the reminder.

'... they haven't reached?' Manoj was saying. Nisha pulled herself back into the conversation. Her sister, who had disappeared for a while, now had a dupatta tucked firmly around her head, leaving just the tip of her hairline exposed.

'They'll be here any minute,' Rupa said. Nisha felt she could hear a hint of pique in her sister's voice, but Manoj didn't seem to notice. She'd always seen her sister as a modern, independent woman, so it was somewhat strange seeing her in this role. Love had funny effects. That first attraction had to be quickly buttressed by pity, a true sense of the other's humanity, a willingness to partake in it. 'Ma is in the bathroom, getting ready,' Rupa said. A flash from just before the wedding, Nisha's mother telling her what they would be buying their oldest daughter to take into the new home: one refrigerator with freezer, one Western-style commode.

'Did you tell Umesh bhaiya that you thought it was me?' Nisha asked.

'What good would that do?' Rupa asked.

'I don't know. Maybe he could take it off the group. Maybe he would have.'

'We tried,' Rupa said. 'But he didn't take the call. When I messaged him, he replied saying he hardly looks at the WhatsApp group any more. He doesn't have time.

One of the members has become the mod. But you know what Umesh's like. Made sure to mention that he was working on something huge. Trying to get into real estate, apparently. With Negi. The MLA.'

'I've been hearing about that too, here in Ranikhet,' Manoj said. 'There's a lot of talk about a big project Negi is putting up.'

For a reason that she could not immediately identify, Nisha began to think again of the GIF, the image of Bharat Mata that seemed to carry her visage. Yes, the AI had transported her to a youthful, prettier version of who she was now, but it was more than the depiction that troubled her. Those two young boys, Muslims, she was guessing, throwing rocks at her feet, at her chest, at her head, blood spattered across the frame, thick drops spurting with her frozen in place like some ghastly, ghoulish fountain. It was this aspect of the image that turned her stomach. To use someone, without their knowledge. Plant this violence in people's minds. Imagine this severity upon the nation. The nation's person. Her person.

'Okay, they're here,' Rupa said, standing. She took the phone in her hand and began to move. 'I really have to go. But I'm not going to let this rest here, Nishoo. Don't you worry. It's clear enough that someone has done this. Someone has used you. Used your photos, your face. I'm going to do something about it.'

That video call had taken place yesterday. *Someone has used you*, Rupa had said. Yet somewhere within she felt used by Rupa too. After all, Rupa had created that online poll without asking, tagged Nisha, posted it, adding to her count some seven hundred followers. It was not the creator of the GIF but Rupa who perhaps unwittingly drew that attention to Nisha's account, to Nisha, provoking the stream of comparisons, compliments, complaints. Unlike many people she knew, Nisha was slightly wary of public posting, but Rupa seemed to have forgotten that. Even when the noise online became overwhelming her older sister had not felt the need to apologize. As Nisha lay in bed, trying to concentrate on the whirring blades of the fan, the agitation she was experiencing, a profound sense of aloneness, of distance from everyone and everything, seemed to get stronger and stronger.

Finding she could no longer lie still, Nisha sat up abruptly. The street light that made its way through the crack in the curtain illuminated the mirror, particularly the glitter on the border of carefully overlapping hearts that a previous tenant had pasted to the aluminium frame. This same girl had put up a decal of Paris on the far wall that Nisha often caught herself staring at: the

Eiffel Tower underneath large stars and a crescent moon, a palace, a bridge, an exact replica of India Gate that she had learned was named Arc de Triomphe. Nisha rose from bed and walked to the shared kitchen for a glass of water. She drank slowly, filled the glass again and returned to her room.

Instead of getting back in bed she began to walk the length of the thick polka-dot rug that lay between the two beds. It wasn't that Nisha was against social media. That would be ridiculous. She enjoyed as much as anyone looking into the lives of friends, family, strangers; she had noted early in her teens how it collapsed the distance between those categories so that strangers could seem as close as a friend or a family member could appear mysterious, unrecognizable from the person she'd known all her life. She loved that sitting here in this small room in this lonely city she could see still the living life of her home in the hills, her cousins on a fishing expedition, the rope swing, girls from her old school making their way along the road to the bus stop wearing the blue-and-white salwar kameez she'd once hated, long posts dismayed at the ever-rising tourist horde on Mall Road down in Nainital, the video of two standing grass snakes intertwined and swaying, apparently making love, snippets that at once warmed her heart and made it sharply pang. Of course, recently many of the posts had been about the forest fires. These were hard to watch, bands of red-gold fire across a dark mountainside, smoke rising high into the night, so that with some posts, shot from the mountain across so they might have caught a dozen of these long lashes of flame, it looked like the world was burning, like all of existence had transformed into hell.

Was it because she'd grown up in the solitude of the mountains, where you could spend hours on a mulchy monsoon path with only the leeches for company, that she felt this aversion to sharing every detail of her life online? That didn't explain why so many people up there, including her sister, loved to post. Back in the hills Nisha had felt her life too ordinary. Their simple home, her clothes, the best of which came from Nainital or Haldwani, the battered Maruti, more than twenty years old, even the holidays they took looked nothing similar to other posts, the posts of city people. Perhaps somewhere she'd felt that she would properly begin posting when she came to the glamorous life Delhi promised. But here, when the initial shock of the city had faded, life settled into an innocuous rhythm, and once again she became aware of the bareness of her room, the stark light of the shop, the deliberate lack of shape to her uniform. She came to see that the reluctance was not about things on the surface. It drew upon something deeper. Nisha knew she could be vain at times. She enjoyed being told she was pretty, she took pictures of herself, many of which she retained on her phone, yet her vanity was such that she would see mostly the unsatisfactory in each likeness, new lines around the eyes, a small patch of scalp, the frightful first appearance of a double chin. It unnerved her that so many strangers could post pictures on the internet with not a care about their flaws – inexplicable people, really, oblivious to what their onlookers might say to one another outside the unrelenting positivity of the visible comments, gleaming and grinning as they showed rolls of belly fat or twisted teeth or skin hammered by acne. The comments below her infrequent posts were invariably supportive, friends, her sister, mother, the boys from school – more guarded in their praise – yet as she looked at the posted rendition of herself she would suddenly become aware of shortcomings she had not before seen. She found herself distrusting the world's reactions, even viewing them with suspicion, as if a collective agenda could be discovered. That was the thing about social media. Even as you were surveilling the world the world would surveil you.

Those video makers were assholes. It was Rupa who should have known better. Though even her intelligent and capable sister could not have anticipated the way those people out there reacted. People saw what they wanted to see. Many agreed with the thrust of Rupa's video. Since the side-to-side comparison showed a remarkable resemblance, it was more than likely the video makers had used her face without permission. Others felt it presumptuous of Rupa to think this of her unknown sister – who the hell was she to put on such airs? – they decided Nisha had the vibe of a snooty bitch in the posts she'd made available online, that she was just another in the long line of people hunting for fame or notoriety on social media.

A third cohort that Nisha slowly identified was also puzzling. Most of them came later to Rupa's post, for some reason. Perhaps the video had been posted to Reddit or some other aggregator. In these comments the outrage had a different direction. They saw the similarity in the two faces, but felt Nisha was being churlish in her refusal of this recognition. She should have been delighted to be elevated in this way, yet she – or her sister – was rejecting the honour. Nisha should have been thanking the creators and AI engine for distinguishing her in this rendition, yet she seemed to be complaining. It was not only an insult to Bharat Mata but an insult to Bharat itself. In the comments they would have their revenge.

3

NISHA HAD RECENTLY TAKEN UP a thirty-day challenge with a YouTube yogi named Tim. Every morning, ideally, she was to click on the link he had sent over email, which would take her to a video where he performed the routine of the day with a large sheepdog by his side. Tim was American and had recently relocated to Hawaii, a fact he made frequent mention of. Nisha enjoyed the routines, which could be performed by practitioners at every level, and even in this febrile moment when her restless mind would not let up those thirty minutes in the morning were something like a redoubt, bringing her to a place where she could face the people at work, though even the prospect of work had become strangely terrifying – now that every customer seemed liable to recognize her, to know the intricacies of her mess.

Tim began each video with a request. 'Try not to look at your phones before the routine,' he would say, with a crinkly surfer smile that reached his eyes, 'social media, text messages, all that.' Nisha knew well why. Sometimes she would pick up her phone from the bedside table with the plan to check her feed for just the few seconds that her body joined her mind in waking, only to find, more often than not, twenty-five minutes had elapsed, that there was no possibility now of both yoga and getting to work on time. It had taken twenty-one mornings to complete twelve days of the routine. At first, she hadn't understood what Tim even meant. How was she supposed to click on the routine if she couldn't use her phone? A little unfair, this American expectation that everyone would have a laptop or at least a tablet as a secondary device.

When she woke that Thursday morning Nisha reached in the dark to the hard plastic seat of the desk chair she used as a bedside table and picked up her phone with the solitary intention of clicking on Yogi Tim's email, only to be halted by an annoyance, a notification indicating she had multiple direct messages from an unfamiliar name, someone called Mayank Tyagi. Her instinct suggested spam, and she went to her inbox to clear out the mess. Suddenly she shivered. Early November, the mornings getting cold. Nisha drew the thin woollen blanket back across her uncovered thigh and calf, the day's yoga routine forgotten, and clicked on the first message.

Dear Ms Nisha Bisht, it began, *I know you don't know me. But actually, I've been following you for some time now.*

Nisha paused briefly to think. This made sense. She had not let in any new followers since Rupa's post went up. Hundreds of requests, perhaps more than a thousand, lay pending. The 'Hidden Requests' section of her inbox was a minefield she had once stepped into, sensing, from the bolded subject lines, both nastiness and flattery on offer. She had not returned. So there was no way the messages came from among the newly curious, their interest either prurient or ghoulish. When had this Mayank followed her? Was there a way of checking? Not that the exact date mattered all that much. Suddenly Nisha remembered obscurely following him back. Perhaps it had been one evening on the way back from work. Cute smile. Had she been trying to make Siddharth jealous?

I came across your account some weeks ago, the DM went on. *There were some travel photos that were very nice. Actually, we were looking for something. It was a work requirement. I was working at the time for a big YouTube channel. We needed to find a suitable face for a new episode.*

Here the first message ended. A sense of alarm had been slowly building and now, at the first mention of YouTube, in fact, the bells rang shrill in her mind. What was this man trying to say?

The second direct message was more scattered. *It was actually my boss's idea*, it ran, *my old boss. Not that I am blaming sir. It is my fault as much as anyone. I would like to say that. The show I was working for was doing a special episode. My boss was very angry. He knew it was a big issue, many people would be angry, we would get lots of views. For the video we needed a very specific animation. But I guess you know all this. We used one of those apps, an AI app. It asked for some suggested images.*

The next message was short: *After that it was our mistake.*

Nisha's eye went naturally to the final message, but for some seconds she did not read, as the breath went out of her. She jumped out of bed, no longer feeling the cold. In her own bed, Shobita stirred, then tossed over, turning her back to Nisha. So this was the guy. The man who'd used her face. Fed pilfered images into an AI application which had rendered her in that new role, mother to the nation, not just mother, embattled mother, struck upon by rock after rock until the veins and capillaries beneath the skin burst, yielding fattened scarlet drops. A victim. Suddenly she could recall with great clarity how she felt upon first seeing herself in that image, how her first thought was of Siddharth, how amused he would be by this recreation, if he were ever to see it, Siddharth who'd departed so swiftly, unaware of her panic at the idea that she was going to become a mother. Nisha was so angry she wanted to reply to this Tyagi bhainchod right away. How dare he? What right did he have? And then to show up in her DMs as if he was fucking boasting. She felt ready to kill him then, as she paced her room, confusing precisely the sequence of things, imagining, though later the truth would resolve in her mind, that this Mayank boy's online appropriation had also chased Siddharth away, sent him skittering out of her life.

Was she going to be late to work? Nisha moved to the kitchenette and heated water for a green tea. She brushed her teeth and bathed quickly, without getting her hair wet. She still felt very angry. When she sat at the dining table to sip her green tea, she remembered the final message. It was as inexplicable as the rest. *Actually, it was my mother*, Mayank Tyagi had typed, *who told me to write to you. Long time ago she was also on the internet. We both were. She thought I should say sorry. I am sorry.*

And there it ended. What had started in the dawn gloom as a brief irritation now felt much larger, like a mysterious foreboding object sitting alongside her. She glanced at her wrist and was astonished at the speed with which she'd gotten ready for once, considering she still had plenty of time before she would have to leave. Boys, girls, men and women of so many different ages had commented or sent messages offering revulsion or congratulation. People said her generation was obsessed with looks but it seemed more like it was the others, those who were older and younger who were so arrested by the flourishing of youth and beauty that they felt compelled to fly into it headfirst, as if they could draw from its power in their own diminished state. And not only today. The cult of beauty had held through history, from before history. Like every person of uncommon appearance Nisha understood this at an instinctive level from an early age, absorbing it as a social reality from small cues that came every day, but the understanding became clearer one summer while she was still in school when a handsome young Palestinian with a flag in one hand and a slingshot in the other had landed on the top of everyone's feed and the front of newspapers across the world, it was like the whole world had started to briefly care for the cause because of the boy, and she'd been taken aback by the power of this appeal, by the history of it, because in the vast proliferation of memes that followed that photograph she had learned about Lady Liberty of the French Revolution and the Old Testament David, vanquisher of Goliath, turned immortal because they were young and beautiful and weaker than that they resisted, people who grew from their own stories to become symbolic of struggle itself.

Suhaan chacha, the rickshaw-waala who took her every morning from the doorstep of the PG to the bus stop, was late. Nisha gave him a call, which went unreturned, but finally he showed up, standing on the pedals to push harder. As they rattled and bumped through the knobbly streets of Kishangarh Suhaan chacha used a grey cloth attached to his shirt to mop the sweat from his face. It was later, as she waited at the bus stop, that her phone buzzed again. A WhatsApp message from Rupa containing an e-paper link in Devanagari. She read the story with an escalating sense of horror. Yet when she was finished, she felt quietly jubilant and very proud. Manoj's story had been accorded front page status, his first, Rupa said, which was another cause for celebration. Nisha marvelled at her brother-in-law's bravery, the bravery of the editor, to take on such a powerful lobby. People must really be angry about the forest fires. This year they had gone on endlessly, overcoming hillsides without intervention by the authorities. They burned still now in November though the dew on the grass would crackle at your touch. So Manoj travelled to the small village settlements around Ranikhet where this year the fires had blazed longest. He spent time with the people who knew these forests best, who lit their own fires to control the vegetation. He helped soothe their suspicion of the media and big city naturalists who liked to portray them as mindless and reckless. The villagers knew how to hold to the natural fire line. But this year nothing had held and neither nature nor man had fought back. After days spent in their company some young men of the village took Manoj to the evidence, blackened cans of kerosene lying amid ruined tree stumps, debris, a careful new fire line unlike any they'd seen before. The major fires had occurred early that summer and the result was the denuded hills that Manoj had now photographed. As Manoj's story detailed, each of these hillsides had remained untouched by so many generations because a long time ago they had been deemed forest land, on which no one could build. But now, late in the summer, forest officials had arrived for an inspection, noted the bare mountainsides and declared that this area was no longer a natural forest, that the zoning could be changed. A major real estate development had been approved. An elaborate plan, as Manoj pointed out in his story, an arrangement that could never have been executed without the connivance of local officials and politicians.

The bus that appeared was thankfully air conditioned. Nisha didn't have quite enough time to wait for the next one. It was crowded, which didn't matter, since the bus ride itself was less than ten minutes. She was happy to stand near the front. As they rode to the bus stop known as Vasant Kunj Police Station she thought back to the first time she'd met Manoj. His close-set eyes had seemed slightly shifty to her, and the expression on his face, as if he was vaguely worried, had also put her off. Nisha feared that he would not be good to her sister, that he would mistreat her in some way once he had her in his home, among his people. She had even suspected he might want something from their family, money or land, though they hardly had any left now. But now she knew Manoj as a solicitous, loving husband, always attentive to what Rupa might want or need, even when they were just hanging out in the house. Nisha could see why her sister, who had always known her own mind, would choose him, choose to marry outside their community though she was beautiful, though she had chosen also to live in the hidebound hills where the prides and privileges of caste and class were in evidence in almost every social gathering. Perhaps it was because of those deeply embedded ideas that Nisha had felt that instinctive aversion which she had now grown ashamed of, which she was glad never to have voiced. Funnily enough, it was in Manoj's eyes that she began to see his kindness. They no longer seemed shifty. As she had gotten to know him better it was as if his face had transformed, turning into a teddy bear version of the gruff visage she'd first shrank from.

And how brave. Manoj's story had detailed the web of connections that could have enabled this to happen, pointing one finger at a very senior forest official and the other straight at the office of the MLA, Negi. For months the offspring of the upper rungs of society in the towns and villages of lower Kumaon had bemoaned the forest fires, posting lengthy laments on social media, but it had taken someone of Manoj's intelligence to put together a definitive attack, something that could really make a difference. She felt proud of him now, as Rupa surely was. Nisha mentally prepared the list of contacts she would forward the story to. Her school alumni group for sure, her old badminton group as well. Manoj had been born into a family that would not have countenanced sending their child to this badminton group, never have tried for admission at the convent school Nisha attended. Yet he was the one who was determined to make things better. To fight for what was right against enormous forces. She should be doing something like this. At that thought her soaring spirit plummeted. Nisha had a sudden sharp awareness of wasting her life, sitting here in Delhi, catering to the whims of the rich and powerful. Had she become a person who thought only of herself?

4

'I'M TRYING TO GET A DZire right away. But the guy only has Innovas. He's asking for seven thousand. That's double.'

'No way. You checked RedBus?' Rupa said. 'It's not like Manoj can go anywhere.'

'I can get a sleeper,' Nisha said.

'And work?'

Nisha made it to the Munirka crossing twenty minutes before the scheduled departure. In her handbag was a folded white paper bag containing a veg burger from McDonald's, fries, two napkins and two sachets of ketchup. In the frantic hours that had just passed after work she had skipped dinner. Nisha had bought the meal planning to eat on the journey but there was a clear window for her to get it out of the way now, there would be no need to make the inside of the bus, especially her little curtained enclosure, smell until dawn of fried oil and mayonnaise. She found a clean spot just underneath the sign for Aggarwal Sweets, sitting on a stone parapet that seemed still warm from the day, placed her overnighter on the ground immediately between her feet, and unpacked her dinner.

She felt angry at herself. The evening hours had been so non-stop at work that she hadn't bothered checking her phone. Her sister's call came at five-thirty, but Nisha only saw the notification when her shift ended at eight. Her mother had also called, eight subsequent times. Not for the first time, Nisha thought about buying a wearable. It would be perfect for when she was at work, for emergencies like this. Rupa sounded destroyed. She'd lost her voice, apparently because of how much she'd been crying. Shouting too, Nisha felt sure. Her sister would be seething.

They had taken Manoj to the emergency room in Haldwani. That was another thing she'd have to remember this time, to get off there, in the plains, before the big white bus commenced the climb home. It would feel strange exiting the bus at that point in the journey after a lifetime of swiftly moving through the dismal little town, but everything was strange now. She hadn't been able to take in quite what her mother was saying over the phone. Who had attacked Manoj? Was that Umesh bhaiya she could hear? Why was he there?

The Volvo arrived. Most of the waiting travellers had bags that were to be thrown in the hold, but Nisha climbed aboard straight away and found the elevated sleeper seat she'd booked. The inside smelled of dinner already, she noted, smiling despite herself, parathas, achar, Mirinda, with wafts also of the thick sticks of incense burning by the driver's seat.

A black Fortuner, its windows blacked out, had been deployed. No one got the license plate. It came up behind Manoj as he was taking his regular morning walk around Sattal lake. The attackers seemed to know the area well, choosing the quietest stretch, where the path bordered a boys' vocational school. The enormous grille of the SUV knocked him off the road. Three masked attackers emerged from the vehicle, following to the point in the undergrowth that Manoj had rolled to. They beat him with sticks, targeting his head first. The hip bone had shattered, and they were investigating for injury to the brain. When Nisha thought about this, the possibility or probability of permanent damage, about how it would affect her sister's life, she felt something like rage bubble up in her blood.

Once the last group had boarded at Akshardham temple and they were moving again there was some urgent conversation from the seats around and a big hand parted the yellow curtain that secluded her, creating a moment of alarm. The man apologized and continued down the aisle, swaying with his bag at his shoulder. Nisha was glad to be able to afford the sleeper. One of the first times she'd done the journey herself, back in college, the conductor had put her in one of the front seats, assuring her he would keep an eye out for miscreants, placing a young kid next to her as added safety. She dozed off a couple hours into the journey. When Nisha started to wakefulness in the dark she found the eleven-year-old boy's hand had snaked under her shawl and was delicately attempting to get under the hem of her T-shirt.

Impossible to sleep tonight, she thought. A message from Siddharth had arrived a little earlier. *Ok have managed*, it said.

'What about work?' Rupa had asked when they spoke, the perfect big sister, thinking about Nisha's career even amidst all that worry. Despite the gravity of the situation Nisha felt very nervous asking so suddenly for leave. Only a few days ago Mrs Jain had come in and given that pep talk and now she was leaving the store in Deven's fledgling hands. Not quite. It was too much for one person, let alone a kid. Maybe Siddharth would be sent back to the store to cover, a thought that gave Nisha a hit of guilty pleasure. More likely someone would be rotated in from one of the other outlets.

Earlier that evening, once she'd spoken to Rupa and resolved what to do, Nisha's first thought had been to call Siddharth. She had not spoken to him at all these past weeks. Perhaps somewhere she had wanted to hear his calm steady voice in this moment of turmoil. She had been cold, however, and matter of fact. Family emergency. Need to go tonight. Don't want to talk about it. Handle with Mrs Jain please. To his credit, Siddharth assented without too many questions. Perhaps he could sense the strain in her voice, the wavering note that suggested she was near breaking point. He would make sure someone else came in tomorrow, that Mrs Jain had no cause for complaint. It could also be that she had inadvertently triggered some latent fear of his own, fear of the card she could play – a teary conversation with Mrs Jain at the next opportunity about how Siddharth had tossed her aside, how he had romanced her both in and out of the shop. Siddharth must know that he had yielded some of his power, that Nisha had claimed some of her own.

It was well past midnight. The bus careened on into the unforgiving darkness. Suddenly her phone began to glow. A call from Umesh bhaiya, of all people. She hesitated, then picked it up.

'Heard you're coming tonight,' he said. 'What time do you get in? I'll have someone wait for you at the bus stop. Just left your sister.'

'She's at the hospital, bhaiya? How is she?' Nisha asked. Immediately she felt annoyed with herself. She needed to be firmer. 'How come you're there? I thought you didn't like Manoj.'

'Your bhinju…' said Umesh, then paused as if considering his words. 'Your bhinju is mad. I told him when he came to Ranikhet, poking his nose. Many times I told him, don't do all this. You're asking for trouble. These people don't play. But does he listen? Mad fucker.'

Nisha wondered if she could detect a note of admiration in Umesh's voice. 'Remember when you used to drive Rupa and me in your Gypsy to that forest near Bhowali to collect pinecones?' she said. 'What was the name of that waterfall?'

'Furbish. Furbish waterfall.'

'That was a beautiful spot.' For some seconds there was silence at both ends of the line. Then Nisha said, 'How could you join up with those people?'

Again that silence. 'My boy will wait for you at the bus stop,' Umesh said gruffly, cutting the line.

Easy enough to blame Umesh for all that he did and all that he failed to do. Yet as the bus swayed around each bend on the familiar road north Nisha began to feel a painful disaffection about her own failure to make any kind of difference. Her brother-in-law lay half dead in a hospital bed and still she did nothing, paralysed by a fear of retribution or notoriety or something else that she needed now to hurdle over. She had to do something, she had to do it right away. Strangely, it was her cousin Umesh's voice that Nisha heard in her mind as her resolve grew about the course of action she would now follow. She went to her account and opened it to the world. Then she started accepting, one by one, the thousands of follow requests that had come to her since the YouTube video first hit the internet. It was quite extraordinary. She was nobody, but all these people had been waiting patiently at her door all this time. In the inbox she saw once again Mayank's messages, so she set a reminder, two weeks, to reply. She was curious about some of the things he'd said. What was that about his mother again?

The bus driver was going alarmingly fast but inside her curtained glowing capsule Nisha felt warm and safe, almost impervious, and brave, stronger than she had in a while. Tomorrow morning she would go to the hospital. Find her stricken sister and savaged brother-in-law, hold them to her. She knew now that she would shoot her own little video. Her first post since the internet decided to make such a big deal out of her face. She would show the thousands of new followers her brother-in-law, the state they'd left him in. She would explain patiently why they had done this to him. She would tell them just who had done it too, as Manoj had done. She had been turned into a symbol, but what did that symbol mean? When it came to it, these leaders who talked about the country as a mother, you might think they would seek to protect, to cherish, but they were just as happy to hurt their mother, to take everything instead of allowing her to give. This is what she would say in her video the next morning. It would bring her a world of pain, perhaps. Not the pain Manoj was in, that was unlikely, but a new kind of difficulty nonetheless. Mrs Jain might admonish her, even fire her. They could make life difficult for her parents.

Nisha thought of her own family. All her life she'd imagined they were just the same as every family in the country, barring a few peculiarities. Maybe that is what we mean, when we call the nation *mother*. We crave the sustenance of her breast. But whatever she gives is not enough. We keep drawing. We never rest, for we fear there is a sibling who receives more.

Yes, this is what she would say in the morning, if her courage held.

ACKNOWLEDGEMENTS

THE OPENING ESSAY OF Sugata Bose's *Nation as Mother and Other Visions of Indian Nationhood* started me thinking about this symbol of our nationalism. After a colleague's recommendation I read Sumathi Ramaswamy's definitive *The Goddess and the Nation: Mapping Mother India*, where I encountered the concept of the geo-body, and so much else.

By coincidence, some years previous, Ms Ramaswamy's brother Sunder had read my application for a job teaching creative writing at Krea University, where I am still employed. He was an excellent presiding presence as I rather nervously began a new career. I am grateful to him, to Siva, Prithvi, Nirmala, the Litt family and everyone else at Krea who has been so kind.

Samir Gadhok read an early draft and answered numerous niggling questions about high-end retail.

My editor and agent, Shruti Debi, incomparable ally. Rahul Soni brought insight, expertise and belief. The team at HarperCollins India have done a wonderful job with the book. Bonita Vaz-Shimray's stunning cover captures so much of what I tried to do with this story.

My son, Agastya, who has changed my life and every sense of what is important.

Most of all I am grateful to Shanta Rana Akbar, mate and guide through these turbulent years. This story would never have found its way without her, and it is for her.

ABOUT THE AUTHOR

PRAYAAG AKBAR is the author of the novel *Leila* (2017), winner of the Crossword Jury Prize and the Tata Literature First Book Award. The book was translated into Hindi, Marathi and Turkish and was used as the basis of a Netflix show.

Prayaag teaches creative writing at Krea University. He lives in Goa with his wife and son.

HarperCollins *Publishers* India

At HarperCollins India, we believe in telling the best stories and finding the widest readership for our books in every format possible. We started publishing in 1992; a great deal has changed since then, but what has remained constant is the passion with which our authors write their books, the love with which readers receive them, and the sheer joy and excitement that we as publishers feel in being a part of the publishing process.

Over the years, we've had the pleasure of publishing some of the finest writing from the subcontinent and around the world, including several award-winning titles and some of the biggest bestsellers in India's publishing history. But nothing has meant more to us than the fact that millions of people have read the books we published, and that somewhere, a book of ours might have made a difference.

As we look to the future, we go back to that one word— a word which has been a driving force for us all these years.

Read.